The Loner

BIANCA BRADBURY

Illustrated by John Gretzer

1970 HOUGHTON MIFFLIN COMPANY BOSTON

Books by BIANCA BRADBURY

Mutt

One Kitten Too Many

Tough Guy

Jim and His Monkey

Two on an Island

The Three Keys

Dogs and More Dogs

Andy's Mountain

The Loner

1

JAY WANDERED past the swimming pool of the Pike's Island Marina, past the restaurant and the office and down the front dock. He had no right to be there. His parents didn't own a boat. That didn't matter though, Jay thought, because he seemed to be invisible. He often came to the marina, and nobody paid any attention to him.

There was nothing invisible about his brother Malcolm. This morning the Great Mal was out there, flying along the river on water skis at the end of a towrope behind an outboard motorboat. His yellow hair shone like gold. The boat flashed across the channel, bringing him close, and he saw Jay and waved a gay greeting.

Jay didn't wave back. Nobody in the world knew

how much he disliked his brother. The truth was that Jay practically hated him.

He didn't bother to look up the next time Mal passed. He leaned on a piling, staring down into the green water, watching the seaweed swirling around the post. There were plenty of people on the dock, but Jay was all alone. Well, he liked it that way.

"Hey, kid!"

Jay glanced up. George Thawless, the dockmaster, was looking straight at him, while he held the nozzle in the tank of a powerboat tied at the gas pump. Jay didn't answer because it didn't occur to him that Mr. Thawless was speaking to him. "Hey, kid!" the dockmaster called again. "Catch the bow line of that boat, will you? I've got my hands full."

Jay woke up to the fact that a craft thirty-five or forty feet long was drifting toward him. A man stood at the controls and a woman balanced on the narrow bow, a line in her hands. She wasn't young, but she looked pretty just the same in her bright blue shorts and halter. She also looked scared. She caught Jay's glance and said, "Please. I'm not very good at this sort of thing."

The dockmaster and the woman didn't know that Jay was the Sharp kid who had two left feet and whose fingers were all thumbs, who never did anything right. She clumsily tossed the line and Jay reached out and, by sheer luck, managed to snag it. He had watched George tie up boats so he knew what to do. He slid the loop over the pile.

The woman just stood there. "Make your end fast to the cleat," Jay suggested. She twisted the line around the cleat.

Her husband leaned out of the window. "Will you take the stern line, too, sonny?" he called. "This wind's holding me off." He left the controls and tossed the line.

It skimmed toward Jay, but it had no loop and it slipped through Jay's hands and landed in the water. Nobody yelled, "Hey, Clumsy!" or "What's the matter with you, Stupid?" The boat owner simply gathered in the line and tried again.

This time Jay's fingers closed on it. He braced himself and pulled the heavy boat in and tied the line, making it fast with a fancy knot which he invented on the spot.

The boat was safe, tight against the dock, and he had done it himself. He stood and watched Mr. Thawless fill the tank, thinking that when he grew up he would be a dockmaster. Let Mal be a lawyer, following in their father's footsteps. Let Mal be rich and powerful. Jay would settle for George Thawless's job.

He came out of his dream world then, realizing the people were looking at him. The woman smiled, holding out a dollar bill. "Here, it's yours," she said. Jay shook his head.

"Go ahead, take it," Mr. Thawless ordered. Jay refused again.

George cast off the lines, explaining to the couple, "The kid's not a regular dockboy. I guess he just hangs around here." The powerful twin engines caught and the boat roared away down river, toward the Sound.

The dockmaster began winding the heavy gas hose on the reel. "Thanks," he said. "I was glad you were around. That's a mean knot you tie. Where'd you learn it?"

"I didn't learn it," Jay told him. "I made it up."

"It was okay," Mr. Thawless said, grinning, his teeth white in his young, tanned face. "Any knot that does its job is a good knot. See you around."

"Okay, see you around," Jay echoed.

He rapidly walked up the dock and crossed the parking space and started along the winding, pebbled road. The world looked different to him and he could appreciate the June sun on his back and the June flowers along the roadside, daisies tangling with clover and buttercups. By golly, he thought, I did something right. That boat needed tying up and I did it.

He began to lose that good feeling as he turned up the shaded lane to his house. By the time he reached the porch he was stepping softly, trying to be invisible. He heard the hum of voices, his mother playing bridge with her usual foursome of ladies, summer residents of Pike's Island. Jay tiptoed past the living room and upstairs to his room.

He had a secret vice that nobody knew about, he kept a diary. He fished it out from under the mattress of his bed.

It occurred to him that if this had been an ordinary day he would probably write for this date, June 23rd,

"Hotshot Mal showed off on water skis." Instead he wrote, "Caught the lines of a big Chris Craft, late model, nice boat. Made them fast."

He wished briefly he had taken the dollar because it would have been the first money he had ever earned in his life. Then he was glad he had tied up the boat for free.

Today was Thursday, so it was Emma's evening off. She worked for the Sharps when they came to spend their summers on Pike's Island. Today she had cooked the dinner before she left, and the boys and their mother arranged their dinners on trays. They often did this on weekdays when they were alone. Mr. Sharp came for the weekend on Friday.

Mrs. Sharp served big helpings of salad. "Did you have a nice day, dear?" she asked Jay. "What did you do?"

Fourteen-year-old Mal didn't give his younger brother a chance to answer. "Mom, you should have seen me!" he bragged. "I've really got the hang of this water-skiing. My friend Larry's going to take me out again tomorrow."

"That's nice, dear," Mrs. Sharp said.

She didn't get a chance to ask Jay again about his day because just then she realized that Mal was shoveling most of the sliced meat onto his plate. She took it back and divided it properly. They carried their trays to the porch.

Jay's mother often said she never got tired of the sound and smell and look of the sea, and Jay felt the same way. He was afraid of the sea but he loved it. Their gray, shingled house stood on a bluff, and from the porch they had a clear view of the Sound, all the way to Littlefield Light. Beyond lay the dark mass of Mosby Island, and beyond that the open ocean, stretching all the way to Spain.

Mal gobbled his dinner down. His mother protested, but he explained that his friend Ben, who was sixteen, would be coming along soon in his car. Jay thought sourly that Mal had as many friends as a dog had fleas. Sure enough, they heard the screech of tires in the drive. Mal grabbed his piece of cake and ran.

Jay and his mother were left alone. He carried the trays to the kitchen, and took out the garbage and burned the papers while Mrs. Sharp rinsed the dishes and stacked them in the dishwasher. "This is getting to be a habit, that boy walking off and leaving us with the work," she said.

Jay didn't answer but he was pleased that his mother was beginning to see the truth, that Mal was a lazy bum who would never do a lick of work if he could get out of it. It was high time his parents caught onto that fact.

The next day Jay went to the marina again but nothing happened. He just hung around. He said hello to Mr. Thawless and nodded to Mr. Towner, who owned the marina. Mr. Towner nodded back but he didn't seem to really see Jay.

That evening Mr. Sharp came on the six o'clock train. Saturday was a busy day. The Holdens, who were old family friends, arrived from the city by car.

Jay's father engaged a fisherman to take Mr. Holden and the boys out for a few hours of deep-sea fishing. Jay didn't want to go but he couldn't think of a good reason for refusing.

As usual, Mal, with his good looks and sunny smile, was the life of the party. As usual, Jay, with his sandy hair and skinny body and narrow, secret face, seemed invisible.

The fisherman took them far, far out, beyond Mosby Island, and dropped the anchor, and they began to fish. Mal latched onto a big blue. He shouted as he worked it to the side of the boat, while the men urged him on with good advice. Nobody noticed when Jay's line went taut. He didn't say a word. He grimly pulled in the line, although it cut his hands because the fish was fighting so hard.

Mal's fish flopped helplessly on the afterdeck. Jay's was bigger, he could see that when he pulled it close. Suddenly he did a crazy thing. Nobody was watching, they were all laughing, listening to Mal's gay bragging about his skill. Jay reached down and jerked the line sidewise, hard. The hook tore loose and the fish darted away. It would have a sore mouth for a while but it would be okay.

Jay wrapped a dirty handkerchief around his cut hand. The blood came through anyway, and his father noticed. "What happened to your hand, son?" he asked.

"Nothing," Jay said vaguely. "Maybe I snagged it on a hook."

8

The others continued to catch fish, but Jay played idly with his reel and line and didn't even try. He had learned long, long ago not to compete with his brother, who was so good at everything, tennis, football, swimming, fishing. Jay disliked all sports.

He wrote in his diary that night, "I caught a bigger fish than loudmouth Mal did, but I let mine get away."

His father wandered into his bedroom before Jay turned out his light. "Jay, I'm sorry today was a bust and you didn't catch anything," he said.

"That's okay," Jay said, giving his father the sidewise grin that was the only smile he ever seemed to manage.

"You weren't disappointed?"

"No. Really, Dad, I had a good time."

"I'm glad." Mr. Sharp hesitated, obviously wishing to establish contact with this shy, oddball son. Jay didn't know how to help him out. Ever since he was a little kid he had found it hard to communicate, even with his father and mother whom he loved. Maybe he was afraid to communicate, afraid it would slip out how he disliked his own brother.

Now he and his father just looked at each other. Finally Mr. Sharp said, "Sleep tight, son," and clumsily patted Jay's shoulder and went away.

On Sunday Jay didn't go to the marina, but hung around the house. The older people read the Sunday papers, and everybody went swimming, and afterward they had a picnic in an oak grove near the beach. Other summer people wandered up and talked to the Sharps and their guests. Mal and Larry and their pals were cavorting on the Sound, out beyond the swimmers, back and forth on water skis.

Mal was a fast learner. He couldn't bother with two skis, he was out there balancing on one. "Look, there's the Sharp boy using only one ski!" people exclaimed. "Isn't he marvelous?"

Jay wandered off alone, past the Point and out of sight. He wanted to practice his swimming where nobody could see. There wasn't much to him, he was skin and bones, but for some reason he turned heavy as lead and sank like a stone when he tried to swim.

This was another of his secrets. His family took it for granted that because he spent every summer at Pike's Island he was probably a great swimmer.

Today, as usual, when he stretched out on his back to float, he sank and swallowed sea water. He floundered back to shore coughing, disgusted with himself because he was so stupid.

He and his mother drove Mr. Sharp to the train that Sunday night, and Jay was sorry to see his father leave.

He wasn't sorry to see Monday morning roll around, however. He arrived at the marina a little after nine. Mr. Towner was standing in the doorway of the store, and nodded as Jay passed. The marina had berths for two hundred boats, and probably Mr. Towner figured that Jay must belong on one of them. Jay walked rapidly down the front dock.

He rounded the turn, where the dockhouse stood at the corner of the T formed by the front dock. A shipment of marine oil had arrived, and George Thawless was unpacking the cartons, stowing the cans on shelves inside the dockhouse. Mr. Towner's voice boomed over the loudspeaker, "You, George, step lively! A boat needs gassing up."

The dockmaster backed out of the small shack, muttering, "I'll never get this job done."

Jay went inside. He finished unpacking the carton Mr. Thawless had been working on, then dragged the others in, opened them, and neatly stacked the cans on the shelves. He broke the cartons down and folded them and carried them up the dock and put them in a trash can.

When he came back Mr. Thawless was still busy as a one-armed paperhanger, for other boats were idling in the channel, waiting their turn to move in to the gas pumps. Jay found an old broom and swept out the dockhouse. He straightened the gear, odd ropes hung on hooks, a box of fuses that had spilled on the floor, miscellaneous boat equipment. He wiped off the sweating top of the ice chest.

He was wondering what to do next when he became aware that a man was calling to him from a boat tied nearby, "Hey, young feller, I need a twenty-pound piece of ice."

"Yes, sir," Jay said. "Right away, sir." He reached for the ice tongs.

2

HE WAS LEANING on the ice chest, wondering how to cut a piece off the big slab, when the dockmaster joined him. Jay explained his problem.

Mr. Thawless jabbed a row of holes with the pick, and a block neatly fell away. Jay carried it to the boat and slung it over the side to the owner, and waited to get the ice tongs back. The man handed him a dollar and told him to keep the change, and when Jay tried to tell him he couldn't because he didn't work at the marina the man said that any kid could use a little change and to forget it.

Mr. Thawless was watching. A lull had come; nobody was yelling for service and no boats were waiting to gas up. "What's the big idea, kid?" the dockmaster asked.

Coming from anybody else, the question would have made Jay stutter and clam up and walk away. He didn't mind it from the dockmaster, though, because Mr. Thawless didn't seem to think he was either dumb or a wierdo. "There isn't any big idea," Jay said. "I don't have anything else to do. I just thought maybe I could hang around."

"You cleaned up the dockhouse."

"Yes."

"Do you want to work here?"

The question Jay had longed for came so suddenly he wasn't ready for it. "Sure, I guess so," he stammered.

"How old are you?"

"Twelve."

The dockmaster grunted. "That was what I was afraid of," he said. "I was hoping you were older and small for your age. We need help the worst way, but the boss won't hire a twelve-year-old kid."

"That's okay, Mr. Thawless," Jay said. "Thanks anyway. Well, I suppose I'd better get home." He started away.

"Wait," Mr. Thawless called. "Hold on a second. What's your name?"

"Jay. Jay Sharp."

"Mine's George. You can call me George. In case you're hanging around here again, Jay, there's one thing you've got to know and that's how to tie a knot. It'll give this marina a black eye if word gets around we tie up boats with bowknots. Here, watch me."

13

He took an end of rope and twisted it rapidly, explaining a square knot. Usually Jay's hands would have been all thumbs, but today they behaved. In a couple of tries he learned a square knot. George showed him a clove hitch then, and that wasn't too difficult either. The dockmaster cut off a length of rope and told him to practice.

"Thanks a lot for showing me," Jay said. He really started away that time, meaning to leave. He didn't want to wear out his welcome. It was probably too good to be true but he suspected that maybe he had found a friend.

He didn't know that the dockmaster had followed until a heavy hand fell on his shoulder. "Did you ever hear that saying, 'Nothing ventured, nothing gained'?" George asked. "Let's tackle the boss."

They passed through the marina store and entered the office. Mr. Towner sat at his desk in front of the wide window. This was where he watched his domain, the docks radiating out from shore, the workshop, the huge shed where boats were stored in winter.

Mr. Towner swung around in his swivel chair. "Boss, you know you're shorthanded," George said. "You still haven't found me the dockboy I need for the summer. How about paying this kid a few bucks a day to help out? His name's Jay Sharp. He's only twelve, so he can't get work papers. He learns fast, though, and he's willing to work."

"You live over at the Point, Jay," Mr. Towner stated. "I've seen you hanging around, and I made in-

quiries. Your father's a rich lawyer who owns a place there."

Jay said the first thing that came into his head, "My father's not rich."

"He's not exactly poor, though, if he owns a house at the Point. We don't mind you hanging around the marina, Jay, but giving you a job is something else. Why do you want to work?"

Jay couldn't give any answer to that. He couldn't say that if he had a job he'd know he was alive. His days wouldn't be just long, empty hours. He had to say something, so he mumbled, "I'll work for nothing if you'll just let me come here, Mr. Towner."

"Don't ever make a crack like that again!" Mr. Towner barked. "Don't admit your work's not worth anything. All right, we'll give you a chance. We can't hire you as a regular employee because you're under sixteen, but we can pay you a dollar and a quarter an hour if you want to come for three or four hours a day, and will step lively and do what the dockmaster says."

The boss turned to Mr. Thawless. "I'll keep on trying to find you a regular dockboy," he said. "I don't think this lad's up to it. He's a rich kid who's taken a notion it's a big deal to have a job, but in a couple of days he'll get tired of it and won't show up. If you want to put up with him until better help comes along, though, that's all right with me."

Jay hastily said, "Thank you, sir," before George spun him around and marched him out.

He started in on Jay the minute the door closed, and he sounded very angry. "I thought you were a kid from town. I didn't know you lived on the island."

A bellow from the gas dock interrupted him, "Hey, George, you've got customers!" George ran.

Jay could have stayed where he was, could have walked off and faded away and never appeared at the marina again. Some instinct made him pick up his feet and lope down the dock after the angry young man he was fast coming to regard as his best friend in the world.

Mr. Thawless had made fast the bow line of a sleek sports fisherman. Jay caught the stern line, and luckily his fingers behaved and the knot came out right the first time he tried it. He took the owner's credit card and handed it to the dockmaster, then carried the slip back to the boatman. He waited until he was given the order, then loosened the lines and tossed them aboard.

From then on, for the rest of that morning, George ran him ragged. The garbage truck arrived, and Jay was supposed to wrestle alone with the heavy containers, rolling them to the truck. The truckdriver took pity on him and handed him a pair of holey gloves and helped with the barrels. Soon the truck was filled with the junk thrown away by the boat owners, and the oily, dirty waste from the machine shop. Jay tried to give back the gloves, but the driver wouldn't take them, and made a loud remark in Mr. Towner's direction about people who let a little kid do a man's work. The boss heard but didn't answer.

Jay kept the gloves on because they gave his hands some protection. He swept out the store, and watered the shrubbery around the office. He was obeying Mr. Towner's order to weed under the shrubbery when an angry yell from George sent him flying down the dock.

What had happened? Why had the dockmaster turned against him? Jay assumed that he must have

17

done something wrong, but for the life of him he couldn't think what it was. He just went on obeying orders as best he could.

At eleven o'clock his stomach reminded him that he had forgotten to eat any breakfast. He had also forgotten to bring any money with him. He couldn't ask to borrow from George, to buy a sandwich and a glass of milk at the restaurant, not now when he was out of favor with his boss. His skinny body needed refueling, and he began to worry how he could get through the day without food.

That worry was removed, for at noon George told him to go home. "I'll tell Mr. Towner to credit you with three hours' work," he said. "Be here at seven tomorrow morning. Probably you summer kids aren't in the habit of getting anywhere on time. You'd better figure on the fact that if you're not here at seven you'll be out of a job. I may not be around, but if you do come you can start right in, cleaning the washrooms."

Jay nodded. George seemed to be waiting for him to say something. "I don't suppose you ever cleaned a washroom," George said.

Jay shook his head. "Then you've got a treat coming to you," George said, and turned away, dismissing him.

Jay's legs were wobbly, he was so hungry, and it took him a long time to walk the mile home. The house was empty, but Emma was out back, hanging up dishtowels. When she came in Jay was rummaging in the refrigerator, getting ready to make peanut butter and jelly sandwiches.

If she had found Mal doing such a thing she would have yelled at him for messing up her clean kitchen, and Mal would have answered her back and made a joke of it. Mal always got along well with the help. She started in on Jay, and he didn't know how to turn it into a joke.

Emma was an enormous, broad woman. She stood with her hands on her hips and glared and said, "Do you think I run a short-order restaurant around here? You clean up that mess you're making, young man!"

Jay would have liked to remind her that it was his father who paid for the food, but he didn't. He said hastily, "I'm sorry," and wiped up the crumbs and put the stuff back in the refrigerator. Then he carried his lunch outside.

He didn't go down to the beach, but hung around the yard. He was feeling really depressed. He thought and thought until his head ached, but he couldn't figure out why George Thawless had changed toward him. What had he done wrong?

Should he go back to the marina? he wondered. He didn't feel like ever setting foot in the place again, after the way the dockmaster had turned on him.

He was just trying to decide whether to mention his problem to anybody, when his mother's station wagon turned into the driveway. Jay sat on the back steps and watched her put the car in the garage. She spotted him and came over. "Hi," she said. "Where were you all morning?"

He blurted out the truth. "I was working."

She was very surprised and interested, and he told her about the job and about his talk with the marina owner. He didn't mention that he was expected to clean washrooms. He did ask her not to tell Mal.

"Why shouldn't your brother know?" she asked. "Jay, I'm so proud of you! I don't want you to over-tire yourself, but I think you've shown great initiative, and it will be grand experience for you. My goodness, one of our boys a real wage earner! Dad will be very proud, too."

"No," Jay said. "Please, Mom, don't tell Dad either, not just yet. We'd better see how it works out." She reluctantly agreed.

Jay changed into swim trunks and climbed down the bank, following the path through bushes and poison ivy to the shore. Farther along, at the Point beach, the Great Malcolm was cavorting on the raft, diving and showing off to some other boys and girls. Jay turned in the opposite direction.

Two girls and a boy, maybe five or six years old, were playing near the water's edge. The tide was coming in, and they were frantically trying to build a barricade to protect their sand castle. Each wave licked closer as it broke. Finally one washed over their sand barricade.

The kids had done a very fancy job, and they looked ready to cry as they retreated and watched the sea ruining their work. "Why don't you build again, up high where the water won't reach it?" Jay suggested.

"Would you help us?" the boy asked.

Jay shook his head. "I haven't got time."

They went ahead, brushing away the dry layers to get to the wet sand underneath, chattering among themselves. They seemed like smart children, and had a story all thought out, who lived in the castle and so forth. Watching them brought back to Jay his own castle-building days, when he was their age. He hadn't played with other children, though. He had always played alone, and made up his own stories.

The girls collected shells and stones, to shore up and reinforce the walls. Jay hunched down on his heels beside the boy, and soon he was helping build walls and battlements and digging out the moat. Maybe it was a silly way to spend an hour but he had a good time.

The boy explained that his sisters were twins, and that they were the three Lane kids. Their family had rented a house at the Point for a month. When Jay finally said, "I'd better be getting along," they thanked him politely for his help.

He went on and reached his favorite place on the south shore, a cove where trees came right down to the water. One big rock rose above the water, and he climbed up on it and did his imitation of a dive, and landed on his stomach. He tried swimming, tried the crawl stroke Mal was so good at. As usual, he sank. What was the trick that kept other kids on top of the water, after they took their feet off the sandy bottom? The lifeguard at the beach would be glad to teach him, Jay knew; that was what the lifeguard was paid for. But Jay couldn't get up the nerve to admit to anybody that he didn't know how to swim.

He didn't see his brother until dinnertime, when he slipped into his place at the table. Emma served Jay a larger piece of steak than she gave Mal, and Jay knew this was her way of apologizing for yelling at him about making a mess in her kitchen. Jay grinned at her and she grinned back.

Mal wasn't dumb. He saw the look they exchanged, and probably he was sore because he had received the smaller piece of steak. When their mother asked as usual, "Did you boys have a good day?" Mal saw his chance.

He scowled at his younger brother. "Jay did," he said.

Their mother was smart, too. She could tell from Mal's tone that he wanted to pick a quarrel. "That's nice," she said, and went on, "I was wondering if you boys would like to go for a drive tonight."

Mal wouldn't be put off. "Jay had a great time at the beach, making sand castles with a bunch of kindergarteners," he said. "Boy, was I embarrassed!"

Jay could have answered back, "Yeah? So what?" If he did, though, that might lead to a fight. After dinner, when their mother wasn't around, Mal might corner him somewhere. Mal was twenty pounds heavier and he was strong. All those sports he was so keen about had given him powerful legs and arms.

He would tap Jay lightly on the cheek and order, "Come on, fight!" He would order and then he would beg, "Come on, Squirt, hit me! Fight back. You've got to learn to take care of yourself."

Jay would refuse and that always made Mal angrier. He would get hold of Jay and pin him down so he was helpless, and force him to admit that he was a baby who liked to build sand castles.

Jay cut his steak, but it tasted like stale putty in his mouth. Someday, he thought, someday, pow! He would land a left in his brother's kisser and it would silence his brother forever.

3

BEFORE JAY went to bed he set his alarm clock for six. He lay with his arms under his head for a while, hearing the familiar summer sound of placid surf rolling up the south shore. He had put off until now the problem of deciding whether he would show up at the marina the next day.

His arms still ached from wrestling the trash barrels. Why should he do heavy work like that? Who needs it? he thought. Why should he leave his comfortable bed tomorrow morning and walk a mile to a place where nobody wanted him? Why should he clean out the dirty old washrooms? Mr. Towner was right about one thing. Jay's father was rich enough so his kids didn't have to work.

The slow rhythm of the sea worked its magic, and Jay fell asleep.

The alarm clock let out a blast in his ear at six, and he sat on the edge of his bed and shivered, scratching his head, still trying to make up his mind. I'll go, he finally decided. But if they throw jobs at me that are too tough or if George Thawless acts like he did yesterday, as though he couldn't stand the sight of me, then I'll quit so fast they won't see me for dust.

He was used to moving soundlessly, and he slipped downstairs to the kitchen and fixed a bowl of dry cereal. He took a dollar out of the change purse his mother kept in the kitchen drawer, and wrote out an IOU and signed his name.

A big red sun was just heaving itself over the horizon, and the grass and bushes glittered with dew. Jay didn't meet a soul as he ran along the country road, crossing the island to the north shore. Fishing boats were moving along the channel that swept close to the front dock of the marina. The early birds were on their way to the fishing grounds, before the world woke up.

Most of the people who kept boats at the marina spent Saturdays and Sundays there; not many slept aboard during the week. It was too early for the hired help to be arriving, and the place was deserted.

The lights were still on in the men's washroom. Jay opened a closet door and found brooms and a mop. A shelf held cans of cleanser and cartons of paper towels. He hesitated. George Thawless was right — he had no

25

idea how to go about the job. Then a horrible thought occurred to him. What if some woman came into the ladies' washroom while he was working there? He would be so embarrassed he would only want the earth to open up and swallow him. And she would be just as upset as he was.

The later it got, the better were the chances that was exactly what would happen. He ought to do that room first, before some woman who was an early riser decided she wanted a shower.

Jay knocked on the door and called in a quavering voice, "Is anybody in there?" He received no answer. He grabbed a broom and a mop and a rag and scouring powder and darted inside and locked the door.

He went at the place like a whirlwind, swept up the litter, hastily mopped the floor, scoured out the washbowls, filled the paper-towel holders. The room didn't look clean by any means, but it looked a lot better and he didn't dare linger any longer. He gathered up his equipment, unlocked the door and slipped out.

He took more time in the men's washroom because he wasn't nervous about a man walking in on him. He really gave it a good polishing. The place looked great, the porcelain clean, the tile floor spotless.

Mr. Towner got out of his car just as Jay finished and emerged. The boss walked in and looked around and said in a surprised voice, "You did a fine job, sonny. Who told you to clean up in here?"

"Mr. Thawless."

"Humph," the boss said. "Did you do the ladies', too?"

"Yes, sir, but that doesn't look so good," Jay confessed. "I got out of there as fast as I could."

The boss chuckled. "I've got good news for you," he said. "Beginning tomorrow, you won't have to worry about doing washrooms. I've hired a woman for a couple of hours a day to do the clean-up chores around here."

Jay swept out the laundry area, gathered up the litter, wiped off the washers and dryers. Mr. Towner watched, occasionally making those "hrumph" noises. Finally Jay couldn't think of anything more to do. "Can you give me my next job, Mr. Towner?" he asked.

"No," the boss said. "Your orders come from George. Lazy beggar, he ought to be here by now. Suppose you and I go over to the restaurant and have a cup of coffee, and wait for the lazy beggar to arrive."

That was where Mr. Thawless found them. He had evidently looked into the washrooms and discovered that Jay had done them as ordered. He scowled, but he couldn't yell at Jay for loafing on the job because it was obvious that Jay was the boss's guest. He just said sarcastically as he left, "Anytime you're ready, sonny, there's plenty of work waiting for you."

Mr. Towner paid the check, and as they walked out told Jay cheerfully, "George Thawless is the best dock-master I ever had, but it's a lot of fun getting a rise out of him. However, he's your boss, so you'd better mind what he says."

Jay found George on the north dock, where the small boats were moored. He was wrestling a heavy, outboard motor off the stern of one of them. He got it loose, and Jay helped him hoist it up on the dock. They carried it together up to the shore. Jay's share was so heavy he was sure he would never make it up the ramp, and his knees kept buckling, but he did manage.

"We need the truck to take this to the shop for an overhaul, but you don't drive," George said. "Why did I hire myself a helper who's too young to drive? Never mind, the world won't come to an end if it sets here for a spell. There's the ice truck arriving, and that's a job that can't wait."

The ice was delivered in huge blocks which the driver slid off the truck to the ground. George took hold of the first block with his tongs, while Jay tried to steer it with tongs from the back. They maneuvered it past the office area and George paused at the top of the front dock's ramp. "This gets a bit tricky," he said. "You take the bow, and I'll take the stern and try to hold it back. Once it starts down the ramp it's likely to take off on its own."

Jay got a good grip on the front. George hooked his tongs into the back. "Easy," he ordered. "Don't let it get away from you . . ."

He was too late. The heavy block had started a slow slide down the ramp. Jay braced himself to hold it but it was too heavy. He jumped out of the way and the block sailed by him, picking up speed. Luckily no one was in the way. It majestically glided down the dock, paused at the edge and landed with a mighty splash in the channel.

Some men were fishing there and one sang out, "Iceberg, ahoy!" They all cheered, watching the cake of ice turn with the tide and begin its journey down river to the sea. A motorboat coming up the channel barely missed it, and the man at the wheel looked very bewildered, and that made the people on the dock cheer even louder.

Jay had ducked into the dockhouse to get out of sight. Now he heard the voice of Mr. Bates, who owned the *Blue Goose*. "Hey, George!" Mr. Bates yelled. "Why don't you pick on somebody your own size? That kid's too small to manage a big hunk of ice like that!"

He and some of the other men helped Mr. Thawless wrestle the heavy blocks down the dock and hoist them into the ice chest. Jay stood by, helplessly watching. He had a feeling that everybody was wondering, "Where did George find such a dumb kid?"

For an hour or so after that things went better. George replaced some of the planks in the south dock, and Jay kept busy fetching what he needed and handing him things. Just the same, Jay felt completely unnecessary. It didn't take much brains to hand the boss a hammer. Several times George left the job to answer calls from the gas dock. Jay tried pounding nails and only succeeded in bending them and banging his thumb. It hurt so much the pain made him sick. He wrapped his thumb in his dirty handkerchief and said nothing when George returned. He thought miserably, I'm not worth the dollar and a quarter an hour Mr. Towner's going to pay me. I ought to pay him for the privilege of hanging around his marina.

One more bad thing happened that day. Jay was raking the area around the refuse cans when George called, "Jay! Mr. Miller's coming in on the *Calypso* and he'll need some help with his lines."

Jay loped down the front dock. The owner was backing the *Calypso* into the slip next to the *Blue Goose*, and Jay tossed the stern lines to Mrs. Miller. She thanked him and suggested he go forward and make fast the bow lines.

The trouble was that Mr. and Mrs. Miller assumed he knew what he was doing and paid no attention. He glanced along the line of boats to see how the others were tied up, then snagged the lines from the piles with a boathook. He fastened them around the cleat on the *Calypso*'s bow, and satisfied that all was well, he jumped to the dock and started away.

A yell stopped him short. Mr. Miller wasn't angry, he was only amused. "Son, the first rule about tying forward lines is to run them under the bow rail," he said. "How come you didn't know that?"

Jay couldn't think of an excuse. He just stood like an idiot with his head down.

"You haven't been around boats much," Mr. Miller said.

"No, sir."

"Here, let me show you." They went forward, and after the lines were properly strung Jay managed to make them fast with the new hitch he had learned. "How come George hired you as a dockboy when you've never been around boats?" Mr. Miller asked curiously.

"I'm not a dockboy, I'm only a helper," Jay admitted.

He knew that the marina was a gossipy sort of place, and he assumed that the *Calypso*'s owner would tell everybody about the dumb mistake he had made. He saw him in conversation with George, and took it for granted that was what the two were discussing. Apparently, Mr. Miller didn't say anything about it, though. George didn't refer to the matter.

At one o'clock he sought out Jay and told him his workday was over. "Do you want me tomorrow?" Jay asked.

"Sure I do. Why wouldn't I?"

"I thought after I lost the cake of ice you wouldn't want me. I mean, a big hunk like that costs real dough."

"Forget it," Mr. Thawless ordered. "Be here at seven." He gave Jay a friendly bang on the back.

Jay thought of asking his mother for her opinion about why George kept changing. One minute he acted sour, as though he regretted hiring Jay and wished he had never laid eyes on him. The next he was friendly. Today he had overlooked Jay's really big blooper, letting go of the ice and losing it.

He found her lying on the chaise longue on the lawn, reading a book. She glanced up and smiled. "How's my working man? How did it go?"

"Okay," he said, and said no more. The habit of clamming up was too strong. He couldn't bring himself to talk about his affairs with anybody.

The next day went all right. A small, elderly woman came to do the cleaning around the office. Her name was Mrs. Sophie Shortley, and she was a real ball of fire. She announced to Mr. Towner that the whole place was dirty as a phoebe's nest and needed a good turning out. She started issuing orders, and pretty soon both Mr. Towner and Mr. Thawless were running all over the place to do her bidding. She demanded Jay's services and George meekly turned Jay over to her.

Jay had a real thing about neatness; at home he kept his room and his belongings tidy and shipshape. He had noticed that the closets and shelves and counters in the marina store were messy. He willingly fell to, to help Mrs. Shortley put the place in order.

Together they started hauling everything out, cleaning the shelves and putting the stock back neatly. The store carried a thousand and one items, screws, nails, paint, brushes, sealers, life jackets, sailing charts — everything needed aboard a boat.

They only made a start the first day. It took them

three days to do the whole job. They ended by scrubbing and waxing the floor and washing all the windows. By Friday the place was immaculate.

Mr. Towner emerged from his office and a grin came over his face, seeing how nice the place looked. Then he scowled. "You two have wrecked my business!" he barked. "I'll never find a thing."

Mrs. Shortley paid no attention, but ordered him to step aside so she and Jay could clean his private office. "Only over my dead body!" Mr. Towner shouted. "Why did I hire you? Who needs a woman around a marina, anyway?"

"You do," she said. "Get out of the way."

George was roaring with laughter, and the mechanics came running from the shop, hearing the fracas. Jay realized then that Mrs. Shortley and the boss were old friends. "Not one foot do you set inside this door," Mr. Towner said grimly. "Not one pinky do you lay on my desk."

"Will you clean it up yourself?"

"Yes, I'll clean it up myself!"

"All right," she said. "I'll give you two days. You'd better tidy it up good before Monday! Now, I want my pay."

She took Jay's arm and marched him into the office. Mr. Towner counted out her money and handed Jay an envelope. Jay was eager to open it but he planned to wait until he was on his way home.

Mrs. Shortley counted her bills and nodded, satisfied. "How much do you pay the boy?" she asked.

"A dollar and a quarter an hour," the boss informed her.

"You pay me two dollars. The boy's a good worker, so next week you'd better raise him an extra quarter."

"Oh, that's all right," Jay protested.

"No, it's not," Mrs. Shortley told him. "Don't sell yourself short, sonny. You're worth a dollar and a half an hour."

Jay started off. Behind him he could still hear the cleaning lady and the boss arguing about how the business ought to be run. Jay felt a warm glow inside. Never in his life had he met grownups like these, who kidded back and forth and included him in their kidding, as though they liked him, as though he belonged.

He heard George's shout. The dockmaster came pounding across the parking lot after him. "Jay, could you come for a few hours tomorrow? I know it's Saturday, but I need you."

"Okay, George," Jay said. "Yes. Sure. I'm glad you want me."

"I guess I acted kind of ornery to you there for a while," George said frankly. "I'd thought I'd stuck my neck out for you and given a job to a rich kid who would be a complete bust. You're okay, sonny. See you tomorrow."

"You bet," Jay said. "See you tomorrow."

4

ON HIS WAY HOME Jay retired into a clump of alder bushes by the side of the road and opened his pay envelope. He found twenty-four beautiful, big fat dollars and some change. He buttoned the envelope in the hip pocket of his old pants and ran on.

This time Emma didn't make a scene about his fixing his own lunch. It was ready for him, his favorite egg salad sandwiches and a tall glass of chocolate milk. Jay assumed his thoughtful mother had given the order. Emma informed him that his father had called to say he was catching an early train from the city, and Mrs. Sharp had gone to meet him. Mal was not home.

Emma sat down and watched him eat. "What in Tophet do you do with your mornings?" she asked.

"The others are in and out, but you seem to vanish off the face of the earth. What are you up to, young feller? I know enough about children to know that when one disappears that way he's up to no good."

"I just hack around," Jay said vaguely.

"Hack around where?"

"Here and there." Jay stuffed the last of his sandwich in his mouth and stood up.

Emma had been working for the Sharps for years, so she felt she had a right to question them. "There's something else," she said. "Wherever you do this fancy hacking around you manage to get your dungarees and T-shirts filthy with grease and ground-in dirt. Look at your hair! You sandy-haired kids ought to wash it every day. Go up and take a bath right this minute. And toss your clothes down so I can put them through the machine."

Jay did as he was told. Bathed and refreshed, he settled down in his mother's chaise longue to wait for his father. He must have fallen deeply asleep, for he awoke to find his parents standing over him. He was so glad to see his father he sprang up and wrapped his arms around him and hugged him hard.

Jay was embarrassed then. He hadn't done such a thing since he was a little kid. His father seemed to like it, though, and hugged him back.

His mother went off to get ready for swimming, and Mr. Sharp sat on the chaise longue and asked what kind of a week Jay had had. "It was okay" was all Jay could say.

He knew it worried his parents that he couldn't talk to them. The family doctor in the city had tried once to pry it out of him, why he had such a hard time communicating with even the father and mother whom he adored. Naturally, a question like that only made Jay clam up worse than ever.

He envied Mal because whatever Mal had on his mind he spilled. Jay couldn't force himself to do it. So when he mentioned that his week had been okay, that was the best he could do. His father nodded, and they sat in companionable silence.

Jay awoke at six the next morning, although he had set the alarm for six-thirty. The light was already glinting through the thin scrub oaks on the lawn. There was no point in his getting up for another half hour. He watched the light patterns on his wall, and he was thinking. Actually he was counting, with a real sense of satisfaction, the things he had learned during the past week.

He knew how to tie two knots, a square knot and a clove hitch. He knew he could manage heavy trash cans. He had learned the hard way that his skinny body was fairly strong. (Mal thought he had putty in his arms but Jay knew now that he had some good muscles.) He had found out he had the nerve to enter a ladies' washroom and clean it, but he was thankful Mr. Towner had hired jolly Mrs. Shortley to do that disagreeable chore.

What else? He knew that when you tied the bow of a boat the lines must pass under the bow rail. He knew that when you got your tongs on a big slab of ice you held on and wrestled it to a standstill — you didn't relax for a second.

What else? Lots of things else. He had watched Bo Brown, the chief mechanic and yard manager, working on motors. Bo didn't mind answering Jay's questions, so Jay was beginning to know something about gasoline and diesel engines.

Jay was learning things that weren't so practical, too. He was finding out that when grownups kidded with him he didn't have to think up smart answers, kidding back. If he just grinned, showing he didn't mind, he, too, could be one of the gang.

He leaped out of bed, eager to get to his job. He pulled on his clothes and slipped downstairs. His mother was breaking eggs in a pan. "Mom, you didn't have to get up," he protested.

"A working man needs a hearty breakfast," she told him.

She drank her coffee while he ate. "Jay, I want to tell Dad about your job," she said. "Please let me, dear. He'll be so proud, he'll bust."

More than anything in the world Jay wanted his father to be proud of him, but a grudging grunt was the best he could manage. "Don't tell the Great Mal, though," he warned.

She hesitated. Then she said, "Your brother has always been a great trial to you, hasn't he, Jay?"

"Boy! You can say that again," Jay burst out.

"I wish you boys could love each other," she said softly.

Jay couldn't let this conversation go on. If he did the floodgates might open and he might spill the whole truth, so his mother would learn at last how much he loathed his older brother. "Mom, are you going to town this afternoon?" he asked abruptly.

"I can," she said.

"I don't want you to go to any special trouble."

"I'd like to go," she told him. "There are a few things Emma needs at the store."

The ship's clock was chiming six bells as Jay arrived at the marina. He was planning to ask George or Bo to teach him how to tell time by the bells. The hands of the outside clock stood at seven. A note on the locked door of the store was addressed to him. "Jay, Mrs. Shortley isn't coming today. Do the washrooms. The boss."

Jay grumbled to himself but he did the job.

On this warm Saturday cars stuffed with gear poured into the marina. The parking lot was soon jammed. Some boats were in the water but some still rested in their wooden cradles on shore, waiting to be put in.

Jay learned there was no human being as unreasonable as a boat owner whose boat was still on land when he wanted it in the water. Every available hand worked feverishly with the tow truck and the great lift, hauling boats, raising them in the sling, and setting them in the water. George, Mr. Towner, and Bo were just about out of their minds. Theirs was a delicate and dangerous job, raising a craft weighing many tons, setting it down as though it was fragile as an eggshell.

Jay had to keep calling George to sell gas at the front dock, and the fourth time he did it George blew his stack. He really used some quite colorful language. Finally he calmed down and said, "Jay, you're going to learn right here and now how to gas up boats."

Jay knew roughly how to take the lines and tie a boat, how to start the gas pump. George showed him how to stamp the slips with the owner's credit card, and where to file the marina's duplicate. "If somebody pays cash and needs change, you'll have to run up to the store. I'll leave the cash register open," George told him. "If you spill gas, be sure and wash off the boat and wash down the dock. But whatever you do, don't call me again. I don't care if you give away the gas and this place goes broke. Don't bother me!"

This happened about eleven o'clock, and for two wonderful hours Jay was king of the gas dock. Maybe he was only twelve years old but he was the absolute boss.

The only fly in his ointment was that the Great Mal didn't show. Of all mornings, why couldn't this be one that Mal and Larry water-skied in the channel? Why couldn't Mal see him now, king of all he surveyed, tying up boats and pumping gas?

Mal didn't show, but others were impressed. The Millers' granddaughter was visiting on their boat. A tiny, blond girl in a pink bikini, she was taking a sun-bath on top of the cabin. Each time Jay passed she called, "Hi," and he answered, "Hi," as he ran by.

Dr. Prince, whose thirty-four-foot Pacemaker was tied at the end of the front dock, had brought his family for the weekend. He had one son, Jay's age. The boy sauntered over and joined Jay at the dockhouse, and they got into conversation. "How come Mr. Towner hired a kid your age for a dockboy?" he asked.

"I don't know, I guess I was just lucky," Jay told him. He saw no need to mention he wasn't a real dockboy, that he was only a helper.

He was beginning to think he might work the whole day when George came barreling down the dock to tell him he could leave. One of the mechanics would work the gas pumps. "Help is coming on Monday," George said. "Some college kid has applied for the dockboy's job. You'd better show, just the same."

"What time?" Jay asked.

"Seven, same as usual."

Jay had some bad moments on his way home. He was very disappointed that Mr. Towner had found a dockboy. How long would Jay hang onto his own job as helper?

He couldn't spend much time worrying about that today, though. He was about to put into operation a project he had been thinking about all week.

A month ago he had gone to a hospital to visit a friend, practically his only friend in the city. He and Howie Evans were in the same grade in school. Howie was usually called Four Eyes because he wore glasses.

When Howie had an attack of acute appendicitis Jay took a bus and went to see him. The gift he took was an ants' nest, covered with glass, and Howie thought it was a great present. He and Jay were both interested in nature, of which they saw very little in the city. Another gift of Howie's had caught Jay's eye, though, and he thought it was one of the finest things he had ever seen. It was an enormous basket of fruit and candies and nuts, covered with cellophane and decorated with a bow of red ribbon.

Jay didn't know why he thought this was the best gift in the world, but he did. He had decided that when he got his first pay he would try to buy just such a basket of fruit for his parents.

His mother never forgot a promise, and after lunch she got the car out and took Jay to town. As they were crossing the Riding Way, the narrow causeway that separated Pike's Island from the mainland, they spotted Mr. Sharp among the fishermen lining the bridge. He was watching his bob so intently he didn't look up when they passed.

"If you're going to the supermarket, you can just leave me anywhere in town," Jay told his mother. She let him out at the first corner.

He wasn't at all sure that a basket of fruit such as he had in mind could be bought in West River, but he was pinning his hopes on Atkinson's, a fancy grocery store that catered to the summer people. He ran all the way, four blocks along Main Street, and was puffing when he burst in the door. Mr. Atkinson knew him by sight, for

Mrs. Sharp often bought items there. "I want a basket of fruit," Jay gasped.

After he got his breath he explained. Mr. Atkinson understood what he had in mind, and luckily he had the materials to build just what Jay wanted. He chose a large basket with a handle, and under Jay's direction arranged melons, oranges, apples, bananas, peaches, pears in a pyramid. He filled in chinks with limes to give green color, and bundles of cinnamon drops to give red. He tucked in packets of gum and imported chocolate bars.

He stood back, surveying the results like an artist studying a painting. "It's okay," Jay said. "It's really great."

"Would you like a horse made of barley candy, to top it off? That would cost a dollar extra."

"How much does it cost so far?" Jay asked. He had his twenty-four dollars with him but was afraid that the basket had already gone over that sum.

"So far it comes to fifteen dollars."

Jay laughed with relief. "Okay. Yes, sure, I want the barley horse, a red one."

The horse was small but it was beautiful, just like one Jay had received in his Christmas stocking many years ago when he was a small boy. Mr. Atkinson carried the whole thing out back to his workroom. He called Jay when it was ready. He had swathed it in sheets of cellophane and tied a huge pink satin bow on the handle. A card was fastened to the bow. Jay carefully wrote, "For Mom and Dad."

Jay hated to see it covered, but he asked the shop-owner to wrap it once more, in plain paper. He handed over his sixteen dollars, and Mr. Atkinson opened the door and Jay staggered out to the curb.

He was sitting beside the gift when his mother drove by and he hailed her. Mr. Atkinson had to come out again, to help hoist it into the back of the station wagon. Mrs. Sharp was sputtering with questions but Jay just climbed in back and refused to answer.

He had sort of hoped the whole family would be there when they reached the cottage, but it didn't really matter that Mal wasn't home. Jay had the audience he cared about. His father was walking up the drive, carrying his fishing gear, when they arrived. He and Jay wrestled the huge basket inside and Mrs. Sharp stripped off the covers and Jay got his reward. They were really stunned.

Mrs. Sharp hugged him and actually cried, and when she recovered she told her husband what it was all about. "I told you that Jay has a job," she explained. "He must have gotten his pay, and he's spent it all on us."

"I have some left over," Jay said.

He couldn't wipe the silly grin off his face. Everything had worked out exactly the way he wanted it. He had earned the gift the hard way. His folks really liked it — they weren't putting on an act. It was a very impressive present, and Jay knew it.

They were still admiring it when Mal walked in. There it stood, on the dining room table, still in the cellophane. The card had been tucked back in its envelope. "Whose birthday is it?" Mal asked.

Jay watched the face of his enemy as he read the card.

"Humph!" Mal snorted. "You must have been saving up your allowance for years, Squirt, to buy the folks a present like this. Or maybe you got it second-hand. I bet it's second-hand fruit, so you got it cheap."

"There's no such thing as second-hand fruit!" his mother said indignantly.

After dinner that night she unwrapped the basket, and they helped themselves. The fruit tasted as good as it looked.

Jay was riding high, really on top of the world all that weekend. He didn't let anything spoil his happiness. He put off until Monday worrying about the new dockboy. He would find out then whether his own job had been pulled right out from under him.

5

WHAT WILL HE be like? Jay wondered, as he trotted across the parking area.

He soon found out. A small car which Jay's sharp eyes recognized as a five-year-old MG tore across the lot and swooped into an empty parking space, and a towering, black-haired bruiser got out. PAYNE UNIVERSITY was lettered across the back of his sweatshirt.

He paid no attention to Jay. Probably he thought Jay was a kid whose family owned one of the boats. He whistled as he started wiping off his car with a rag.

Jay got his big, stiff broom from the closet in the men's room. He knew where the store key was hidden. He sort of swaggered as he marched past the new dock-boy and his great MG, unlocked the store, and proceeded to sweep out.

"Hey, who are you?" The newcomer stood in the door.

Something pretty good had happened to Jay on Saturday when for two hours he had run the gas dock with no help from anyone, and had made no mistakes. He wasn't just a nothing. Any kid who could present his parents with a sixteen-dollar basket of fruit wasn't just a nothing, either. A couple of weeks ago if he had been addressed by a man who was probably a college football player, Jay would have wilted. He would have mumbled something and just faded away. Now he looked the fellow in the eye and said, "I'm Jay Sharp."

"Do you work here?"

"Yes."

"Then I guess George Thawless needs help worse than I figured," the man said. There wasn't any sting in his words because he was grinning goodnaturedly. "I'm Hank Thompson. Mr. Towner hired me to work the docks."

"Yes, I know," Jay said. He had half a mind to add, "If you want me to, I'll show you how things work," but he didn't. Besides getting more sure of himself he was also getting smarter. He just said, "See you around," and went on with his own work.

The rest of the help arrived, the boss in his big Cadillac, George in the marina pickup with Mrs. Shortley on the high seat beside him, Bo and the electrician and the machinist and the others who ran the shop. Hank took charge of the gas dock.

As the morning went on, it became obvious to Jay that he wasn't really needed anymore. He made himself useful, just the same. He was trying to put off the evil moment when the boss or George noticed him and fired him. He cleaned the men's washroom while Mrs. Shortley did the ladies'. He folded a large pile of empty cartons and jammed them into a trash barrel. Then he crawled under the ornamental bushes which surrounded the store to finish the weeding.

Suddenly the loudspeaker let out a bellow. "Jay Sharp!" There was a pause, then Mr. Thawless's growl. "Where is that confounded kid?"

Jay scrambled out. George was standing in the doorway, not ten feet away. "Bo needs you," he said.

For the next hour Bo kept Jay busy in the shop, filling barrels with empty oil cans, giving the place a general cleanup. Bo was a genius with engines but he had one failing — he was a messy workman. He left tools all over the place. He lost his temper when he needed a tool and couldn't find it, even when he himself had misplaced it.

This morning he took the trouble to explain the system to Jay, how the tools were supposed to be hung on the shop wall or put away in cupboards and drawers. When he finished he said, "Now you know what to do when I say, 'Put the tools away.'"

Bo took it for granted, apparently, that Jay was to be kept on. Feeling somewhat surer of himself, Jay did a careful job, wiping the tools clean and arranging them, scattering sawdust to soak up oil spilled on the cement floor of the huge, barnlike shop, sweeping up the sawdust and litter.

He was just finishing when Mr. Towner entered, blinking because it was so dark inside, after coming in from the bright sunlight. He had a disgusted look on his face. "As though we don't have enough real work to do for these boat owners, we have to keep track of their animals, too," he said. "Jay, Mrs. Farnum has lost her Pekingese. Somehow it got off her boat and disappeared. Will you try to find it for her? She's having hysterics in my office."

The workmen roared with laughter. "So you think it's funny?" the boss barked at them. "I can't go back to my office until that woman's confounded dog is found!"

Jay ran to the office. Mrs. Farnum was walking up and down, wringing her hands, and sure enough, tears were running down her face. She seized Jay's arm. "Boy, I'll give you a hundred dollars if you'll find my Toodles!" she cried.

He managed to escape her grasp and told her he would do his best, and set off. He began making his way up and down the lines of parked cars calling, "Here, Toodles, here, Toodles!" Why couldn't the dog's name be Mutt, or Duke, or something sensible? he wondered.

He came to the end and was starting on the next line of cars calling, "Here, Toodles!" when he ran right into Eddie Prince, the boy he had visited with for a while that morning when Jay was king of the gas dock. "Who's Toodles?" Eddie asked.

"It's a stupid dog that belongs to Mrs. Farnum, over on the east dock," Jay explained.

"Is it a Pekingese that looks like a fancy dishmop?"

"That's the one. How about helping me?"

Jay spoke before he thought. It was hard for him to talk to boys his own age, and he expected a turn-down now. He was very relieved when Eddie said, "Sure, why not?"

Eddie took a section of the parking lot and started calling, "Here, Toodles! Where are you, you silly dog?" When he and Jay met again by the swimming pool he complained, "Why couldn't she give her dog a decent name? I feel like an awful fool."

"Me, too," Jay told him.

They had covered the marina area thoroughly, so they started along the road that led across the island. Eddie talked about his cousin's dog, which had a sensible name, Sergeant. Jay admitted that he himself had never owned a dog. They walked along together talking about dogs, and what kinds they liked, and there wasn't any strain and Jay almost stopped short because the thought occurred to him, Hey, maybe I've got a friend.

He didn't want to muff it and lose a friend even before he was sure of him. At home, Mal talked all the time about sports, and Jay always kept mum. Now Eddie started talking about baseball, and what teams had the best chance of winning the pennants. What Jay knew about baseball he could put in his eye but he went along, agreeing, "Yeah, sure," with whatever Eddie said. He was thinking that maybe he ought to read the sports page in the newspaper and find out what baseball was all about.

They looked in the yards along the way and saw plenty of other dogs, but never an apricot-colored Pekingese. They asked everybody they met. The road they were on forked, the right going to the Point, where Jay lived, the left leading off the island. If the dog had turned right toward the Point, they would have a long search but they would find it. If it had turned left toward the Riding Way, they would be in real trouble. Once Toodles reached the mainland, their chances of finding her would be slim.

They were nearing the Riding Way when they saw a woman hanging clothes in her backyard. She had good news. "Yes, a silky little dog came through here not five minutes ago," she said. "It was with another dog, a mixed breed, and they went across the lots toward the woods." They thanked her and ran.

Soon they heard barking ahead. They stumbled into a tangle of brambles, and both were badly scratched by the time they reached a cleared space, under tall trees. Toodles was there. A long-haired brown dog sat, panting, while the Pekingese frisked around, begging him to play.

The brown dog dropped its tail and moved warily off when the boys called to him, but Toodles hesitated. Jay and Eddie had to sit on the grass for a long time, calling her idiotic name, until finally she came within arms' reach, and Eddie grabbed her.

She struggled to get away, and Eddie had an awful time holding her. "We're a real bright pair, we didn't bring a leash," he pointed out. "We'll have to use your belt."

Jay's belt had broken, so that morning he had threaded a piece of rope through the loops of his dungarees. "I'll lose my pants," he protested.

"That's okay," Eddie said. "It's better you lose your pants than we lose this confounded mutt again. Hurry up! I can't hold her much longer."

The brown dog trailed a hundred yards behind them on the long walk back to the marina. Toodles fought the rope, trying to get free. Eddie had to lead her, for Jay was much too busy trying to keep his pants on.

Mrs. Farnum saw them coming and rushed to meet them and gathered her precious baby in her arms. She asked the boys to walk with her to her boat. She got out her checkbook and they realized she actually intended to pay them a hundred dollars, as she had offered.

They refused. "It wasn't worth that much," Jay told her.

He really put his foot in his mouth when he said that. "My precious Toodles is worth ten times that amount!" Mrs. Farnum cried.

"I wasn't insulting your dog, I just meant we didn't earn it," Jay said. "How about a dollar apiece? That's plenty."

"Would you each take five dollars?" she asked. They agreed.

Toodles whined as the boys set off along the dock, and Eddie turned back. "Your dog needs more exercise, Mrs. Farnum," he said. "You ought to walk her more. Then she wouldn't act so crazy and run off, when she gets loose."

"Would you boys do it, if I paid you for your time?" she asked. "I know my baby needs more exercise, but I'm not as young as I once was, and it's hard for me to get on and off this boat."

Jay told her he already had a job, but Eddie agreed that every morning and afternoon he would report for dog-walking duty.

Jay didn't hang around while they settled the details because he had been away for a long time and was afraid George would be angry. George and Mr. Towner had been watching from the office window, though, and they weren't sore at all, they were delighted. "Now we'll get some peace around here," George said. "Mrs. Farnum had the whole place in an uproar."

It was noon, Jay's quitting time, and George told him he could leave. Jay didn't ask if he was wanted back the next day — he had no desire to put ideas in his boss's head. He came out of the store and found Eddie hanging around, waiting for him. Eddie asked where he was going.

"Home," Jay said. "I'm through for the day."

"Oh."

Jay didn't ask Eddie to visit him at his house. He wanted to. He would have liked to say, "Hey, why don't you come to my house this afternoon?" but he didn't dare. Eddie might have turned him down. Or, if Eddie did come, Mal might be hanging around the house and Mal might make cracks, running Jay down, making him look like a fool or a baby. Jay couldn't remember Mal ever exactly doing such a thing, but being the kind of a brother he was, he well might.

Jay hesitated too long. Finally Eddie said, "Okay, kid. Will I see you tomorrow?"

"Sure," Jay said, relieved. "I'll see you tomorrow."

6

HE WAS HALFWAY HOME when he discovered he was being followed. The brown dog which he and Eddie had met in the woods was trailing him, keeping to the side of the road and ducking into the bushes each time Jay looked back. When he reached his yard he waited outside for a while, but the dog didn't appear.

He saw it the next morning on his way to work. It lay under a bush, back from the road. He held out his hand and the dog thumped its shaggy brown tail on the ground. It got to its feet and started toward him, but a few feet away it stopped, refusing to come nearer.

Jay had had no experience with dogs. He wanted to make friends with this one but had no idea how to go about it.

That noon he stopped at the marina restaurant when

he finished work, and bought some doughnuts to eat on the way home. He slowed his steps as he approached the bushes where he had seen the dog earlier that day. Sure enough, there it lay, its nose on its paws. Jay ordered, "Come here," and held out a doughnut.

The dog eyed the food longingly, but did not advance. Jay left the doughnut on the side of the road and went on, and when he reached a bend he looked back. Both the food and the dog had disappeared.

Jay's games were always solitary ones, and now he started playing a game with the dog. He was sure it had no home, for with each passing day it looked thinner. Each morning Jay swiped some tasty tidbit from the refrigerator, a piece of meat or some leftover spaghetti or just buttered bread, and left it on a piece of waxed paper at the spot where the dog had taken the doughnut. Each day when he neared the next bend and looked back, he saw the dog gobbling it down.

Jay's mother didn't often try to force him into a conversation, because it was such uphill work. One night that week, though, she came to his room, because his light was on and he was reading. "What's the matter, son, can't you sleep?" she asked. "It's after midnight."

"I was going to put the light out in a minute," he said. Then, because his mother looked so pretty in her blue robe, with her hair tousled, he smiled.

She sat on the edge of the bed. "You seem happier this summer," she said.

"I'm having a great summer," he told her.

"Do you mean it?"

"Yes, I mean it."

"Is it because of your job?"

"I guess so." He would have liked to tell her all about it, about his new friends, Mr. Bo Brown and Mrs. Shortley and Eddie, about how good his bosses were to him, and how he was just hanging on to the job by the skin of his teeth because he wasn't really needed now, but nobody had yet fired him. He couldn't. The habit of keeping mum about his affairs was too strong.

She waited, but he didn't go on. "You don't seem to like your brother any better, though," she said. "Jay, I can't tell you what it would mean to your dad and me if you boys could be friends. Both of you are so wonderful. Dad and I have often thought that if we could only shake the two of you in a bag, so your good qualities would rub off on Mal and his on you, then you'd both be perfect. I know he's a trial, and he does bully you sometimes, but Jay, have you ever thought that maybe you're a trial to him, too? I mean, it wouldn't really hurt you to show an interest in sports, in the things Mal's so keen about."

"Who needs it?" Jay mumbled.

His mother sighed. "Maybe in time you'll get to be friends," she said. "It's a comfort to me that even if you don't get on, at least you don't hate each other."

Jay suddenly felt sick. He loathed having to talk about his feelings. Just once, though, it might be a good idea to speak the truth. People hedged, and dodged, and never spoke the truth if they could help it. "I do hate Mal," Jay said harshly.

"Oh, please, darling, don't even think such a thing," his mother begged. "It's not true!"

Jay had to stop this intimate talk somehow. He saw the hurt in his mother's eyes, and wished with all his heart he had never mentioned how he really felt toward Mal. "Shhh, Mom," he whispered.

For some time he had been hearing an odd sound outside, in the dark. His mother kept still, listening, too. It came again, a soft sound, like a moan or a whimper. Mrs. Sharp moved to the window and Jay snapped off his bedside lamp. The moonlight was so bright they could see that the lawn was empty. "There's nothing there," she said.

"Yes, there is; it's a dog," Jay told her. "I meet it on the road, and it's been hanging around for several days. Mom, do you mind if I put out food for it? Could I give it some of that meat pie that was left over from dinner?"

"Let's do it," she said. "Let's give it a nice meal."

Jay was surprised, for she seemed pleased with the idea of sneaking down at midnight to fix food for a stray dog. It occurred to him he didn't really know his own mother very well. He had really expected she'd say No. They went down together and she carried the dish out and set it on the back steps, calling softly, "Here, dog, come, dog."

It didn't appear while they waited. "Let's watch from your window," she suggested.

They stole through the silent house and stood at the

window, watching. Soon the brown dog crept from the rhododendron bushes, crossed the lawn, and ate the food. It stood for a moment staring at the dark house, then trotted off.

"That was what kept you awake," Mrs. Sharp said. "You were worried about the dog. Now you'll sleep. Good-night, dear." She kissed him and went away.

She got up the next morning to make his breakfast, and handed him a paper bag as he was leaving. "This is for your dog friend," she said. "Emma's been complaining because food was missing. She'll just have to go on complaining!"

This was on Friday. All week Jay had been trying to make friends with the shaggy dog, and he was getting discouraged. He spread out the paper with the tasty scraps his mother had donated, and as usual, the dog emerged before he reached the bend in the road. It wagged its ragged tail while it ate.

Jay turned back. "Here, boy," he called, snapping his fingers. The dog took a few steps, obviously wanting to obey, but stopped ten feet away. Jay couldn't waste any more time, and went on.

He had a few fixed duties now, such as sweeping the huge repair shop and sorting and putting the tools away and cleaning the men's washroom and emptying the trash barrels. People called him "the odd-jobs boy," and he was at the beck and call of whoever needed his services.

He was acquainted with dozens of boat owners and

their families, and when he ran along the docks people called, "Hi, Jay!" after him. He was finding it easier to talk to people.

He and Hank, the dockboy, were getting along great. Hank called him "Squirt," and "Shrimp," and sometimes they had real talks when Jay had a few minutes to hang around the gas dock. Hank was a college junior and played varsity football, but Jay didn't hold that against him. Hank didn't try to ram sports down Jay's throat the way Mal did, and he could talk about other things, too. Jay had let slip the fact that he had an older brother who played football, but Hank didn't say, "I suppose you'll follow in your brother's footsteps and play, too." He accepted Jay for himself.

Of course the most important person at the marina was Eddie. He and Jay saw a lot of each other. Jay was wary, though, because in the past he had made what he had thought were friendships but they had always fizzled out. Sooner or later other boys found out that Jay was sort of a cipher who had no skills and was about as communicative as a clam buried in the mud. Jay fully expected that another boy would appear on the scene, and Eddie would lose interest in Jay and drop him like a hot potato.

It rained that Friday. The others at the marina wore foul-weather clothes but Jay had none and it didn't matter to him that his T-shirt and shorts got soaked through. He did his work and quit as usual at noon. He bought two doughnuts and started home.

At the spot where he and the brown dog had their

daily meetings he sat down on a wet rock under a scrub
oak and waited. The rain had turned to a drizzle, then
stopped. Soon Jay heard the bushes behind him moving, but he didn't look around. He didn't jump,
either, when a wet, cold nose was suddenly pushed into
the crook of his elbow. He sat perfectly still until the
dog moved around in front of him.

It was within reach, but Jay didn't grab it. He just
said, "Hi, Major," which was his private name for the
dog. He offered a piece of doughnut and Major took it,
and Jay ate a piece. They shared the doughnuts until
they were gone.

The dog sat quietly beside Jay until Jay put out his
hand, and then it began to tremble, fright clouding its
eyes. Those eyes were dark brown, flecked with gold,

and it seemed to Jay he had never looked into more beautiful ones. He succeeded in laying his hand on top of Major's head, and gently began to rub the dog's ears, and run his hand down its neck and then down its back.

Major seemed terrified to be touched, and yet he wanted to stay and be petted. It occurred to Jay that probably somebody had beaten him, beside starving him. How long the two sat there Jay didn't know, but when he stood up and said, "Come, Major," Major followed him home.

Jay had no idea how he was going to put over the fact that he intended to keep the dog. He didn't dawdle when he reached his driveway; he didn't take time to plan any sort of campaign. Major was jogging along at his heels, and stopped short when they reached the back door. Jay seized his chain collar and pushed him inside.

Emma was at the stove. Jay's mother was spreading sandwiches at the table, and Mal was sprawled in a chair, eating the crusts as she cut them off. Jay announced in a loud voice, "I'm going to keep this dog."

Emma's face darkened. Mrs. Sharp's brightened, and she exclaimed, "Oh Jay, you caught him!"

At the sight of strangers Major shrank back, his eyes wild. "Where'd you get that mutt?" Mal demanded.

"I don't think he's so bad," Mrs. Sharp said. "I never did get a look at him, last night. After he's bathed and combed I bet he'll be a fine-looking dog. Suppose you tie him outside, Jay, while we have lunch."

Jay felt so grateful to her, tears came to his eyes. He cut off a length of clothesline and tied Major near the door. When he went back in Emma was scowling and announcing in loud, clear tones that no dirty dog was going to mess up any house she worked in. Jay suspected, though, that Emma's bark was much worse than her bite and he didn't have to worry about her.

He knew for sure he didn't have to worry about his mother. He was finding out that she wasn't lined up against him on Mal's side, in the constant war between the brothers. Besides, he was beginning to believe that she had a real nice feeling for animals. He had never happened to see this side of her before.

Emma soon left. She was taking the rest of the day off to visit a cousin. The three Sharps sat down to lunch and Jay braced himself, waiting for Mal to make the crack that would open the battle. Through the door Jay could see Major curled down on the grass, watching the house.

Oddly, Mal sounded quite mild. "Ye gods," he said. He, too, could see Major, from where he sat. "Mom, if we're going to have a dog, can't we get a decent one? Maybe Dad would get a German shepherd or a collie, something that looks like a real dog."

Jay didn't have to reply, for his mother came to Major's defense in a spirited way. "Spending money doesn't always get a good dog," she said. "When I was a young girl my father brought home a puppy that had all sorts of breeds mixed up in it, and it was the best dog that ever lived!"

"That one out there is scratching itself," Mal observed. "It's probably covered with lice and fleas. You keep your mutt out of my bed, Squirt! That would be a good name for it — Mutt."

He got up from the table, saying indifferently, "It's no skin off my nose if you want to let Jay keep that homely mutt, Mom."

"He's right about one thing," Mrs. Sharp said, after Mal was gone. "Probably your dog is riddled with fleas, and he ought to be checked over by a vet. Suppose we take him this afternoon."

They ran into a snag when they arrived at the veterinarian's. Dr. Brooke turned out to be quite young, and he was very serious about his job. He looked Major over and decided he was in fair shape, although he was too thin and needed good feeding and vitamins. While he was bathing Major with flea soap he found several ticks around Major's neck and chest, and removed them. Then he asked, "Where did you get this dog?"

Jay explained that Major was a stray he had made friends with. "How can you be sure he doesn't belong to somebody?" Dr. Brooke asked. "How do you know his owner isn't looking for him? Hadn't you better call the dog warden and inquire?"

Jay's heart sank. His mother asked Dr. Brooke to make the call.

The doctor's conversation with the warden was a long one. Once he broke off to ask Mrs. Sharp her telephone number. When he finished he explained, "By law, you ought to turn the dog over to the warden. He says nobody has reported losing a dog that answers this one's description. Just the same, the warden's supposed to keep it at the pound for a week. At the end of that time, if the owner hasn't turned up, you could adopt it by paying five dollars, the legal fee. The warden's a good man, though, and he doesn't insist on picking it up and holding it at the pound. He's agreed to let you keep it. Of course you'll have to give it up if anybody claims it within a week."

"He must be a fine owner if he's not interested enough to report it missing!" Mrs. Sharp exclaimed indignantly.

"The chances are he deliberately stopped and pushed it out of his car, in order to get rid of it," Dr. Brooke told her. "It's sad but true, that happens all the time, cats and dogs, puppies and kittens being dropped from cars. I'd say this is one of the lucky ones, to find such a good home."

7

MRS. SHARP went alone to meet her husband that evening when he arrived on the six o'clock train. Jay figured she wanted to break the news about the new member of the family.

He hung around the backyard waiting, getting more nervous by the minute, planning how he was going to argue his case. Any kid who had a lawyer for a father had to assemble his arguments carefully.

He needn't have worried. His mother must have done a good selling job, for when Mr. Sharp saw Jay he called, "I hear we've got a dog!"

Major cowered when Mr. Sharp held out his hand. "It looks like a nice one," he said. "You'll like me, fellow, when you get used to me."

"It's easy to see that right now he's a one-man dog," he added. "And you're the man, Jay."

At dinner the whole conversation revolved around Major. Emma put in her two cents' worth while she was passing the plates, after Mr. Sharp carved the roast. "You'd better make sure that dog's tied outside tonight, sonny," she told Jay. "His life won't be worth a plugged nickel if I come tomorrow morning and find out he's not housebroken."

"You bet, Emma," Jay said.

"You know who'll clean it up if he does mess up the place, don't you?"

"You bet, Emma."

"Emma, I don't consider this a proper subject of conversation for the dinner table," Mr. Sharp protested.

"All right," she said, "just as long as your son and I understand each other."

Mal seemed restless. Maybe he was bored with the conversation, or maybe he decided that since Jay had acquired a dog it was his turn to get something, too. Emma set a deep-dish apple pie in front of Mrs. Sharp to be served, and left the room to fetch the coffee. "Dad, we've been talking about buying a boat," Mal announced abruptly. "Don't you think we ought to do it this summer?"

He hadn't led up to the subject tactfully, and his father looked startled. "I don't know," he began.

"Dad, every other kid on the island has a boat!"

"Every kid?"

"Well, almost every kid. I have to sit around and

wait for Larry or somebody to ask me if I want a ride. I don't get to do hardly any skiing. If I had a boat the other guys could run it and I'd get some practice."

His parents didn't answer right away. "I notice Jay didn't run into any opposition when he brought home that mangy dog," Mal pointed out.

"What kind of a boat did you have in mind?" Mr. Sharp asked.

"Dad, that's great if you want to talk about it!" Mal exclaimed. "I figure we ought to get a fiber glass runabout, maybe eighteen feet, big enough to take a thirty-five horsepower motor, or even a fifty. It has to have a heavy motor so it'll go fast enough to pull a skier."

His father made no comment. "If you don't feel like putting out the money for a new one, a used one would be okay," Mal went on. "There's a nice little runabout at the public dock in town that has a For Sale sign on it. It's a couple of years old but it looks good."

"Have you seen the owner? Have you found out how much he's asking?"

"Yes, I saw him. He works at the gas station near the town dock. He wants four hundred. That's a bargain."

"That's a lot of money, son. If you were working, and earning part of the price, I'd feel better about such a proposition."

"Where would I get a job?" Mal asked. "Believe me, Dad, if there were any work jobs on the island, I'd get myself one."

The three looked at each other. Jay had sworn his

71

parents to secrecy but he saw that they wanted him to tell. "I didn't have too much trouble finding a job," he said.

He might as well have tossed a live bomb on the table, the way Mal reared back and exploded, "You think you're pretty funny!"

Nobody spoke. Mal began to look uncertain. "No kidding?" he asked. "Is that where you go mornings?" He must have realized he didn't look too good. "I didn't pay much attention," he mumbled. "I figured Jay spent his mornings playing sand castles with his kindergarten pals."

"Mal, didn't you wonder where Jay got the money to buy that beautiful basket of fruit?" Mrs. Sharp asked.

"I thought he saved up his allowance."

"Tell him, Jay," Mrs. Sharp ordered.

"You've seen me over at the marina. I'm the odd-jobs boy there," Jay explained. "I run errands and clean up the place and help tie up the boats. Sometimes, when they're shorthanded, I sell gas."

Mal looked more than impressed, he looked stunned. Jay began to get carried away as he went on, "When those forty-foot boats come up to the dock it's quite a job to get their lines and make them fast. The boat people are okay, they give big tips. Sometimes a dollar."

"You make it sound so good I wish you'd get me a job at the marina," Mr. Sharp said with a chuckle. "It sounds better than the law business."

That was the end of serious conversation. Mal didn't bring up the subject of boats again. Actually, he didn't say a word.

After Emma had cleaned up the kitchen and gone home, Jay's mother suggested that he bring Major inside. The family gathered in the living room to watch TV. Jay brought in an old beach blanket and spread it beside him on the sofa and set Major on it. The dog trembled and crowded as close to Jay as he could get.

Jay needn't have worried about his dog being housebroken. Twice during the evening he took Major outside. Major did what he was supposed to do. Before they went up to bed Jay took him for a long walk along the dark road.

Major slept on Jay's bed. Jay would never have dreamed he would ever get to sleep with his own dog and he found it was just as great as he could have imagined it. Every time he stirred, Major woke up and sighed a deep, happy sigh.

At dawn Major waked Jay by jumping off the bed and jumping back on again. Jay pulled on his sneakers and pants and they went outside. It was queer, walking around in the gray dawn, queer and nice. They were strolling along the beach when the red sun popped up out of the sea.

Jay fixed the same breakfast for both, cereal with milk and sugar. His mother came down at seven, and he was glad he could tell her, "Emma didn't need to worry. Major didn't make a single mistake."

"He's not going to be very happy here after you go to work, but I'll do my best to keep him entertained," Mrs. Sharp promised.

Major was on Jay's mind all morning. He worried about how his dog was making out, and he also worried about what Mal planned to do. Naturally, no older brother could let a younger one get away with what Jay had done last night, playing the big shot and bragging about his great job. All brothers were enemies, weren't they? Mal would have to get even somehow.

Eddie hung around with Jay most of the morning. He now had six dog-walking jobs, and was earning a nice bit of cash. He was on call, for his clients were likely to get the urge at any time. When he was free, though, he sought out Jay.

Jay didn't want to start liking Eddie too much. He would only build himself up to a big letdown, because his friendships always busted up, sooner or later. It was hard, though, not to like Eddie, with his frank air and his friendly grin.

That day the ice truck came late. Hank Thompson took charge of getting the huge cakes down the dock, with Jay in front to guide them. Eddie followed after, bringing Bingo back from his morning walk.

Bingo, an enormous Great Dane, was Eddie's most difficult client, because he never walked, he either lunged or loped. Marina people enjoyed the comical sight of Eddie, red-faced and sweating, being jerked along, or flying through the air, at the end of Bingo's leash.

Bingo lived on a yacht that was too big for any of the slips and had to be tied outside the front dock. Eddie delivered the dog to its owner, and after that he was free. He joined Hank and Jay, who were chipping the blocks to fit them into the ice chest. "Wow!" Eddie said, helping himself to a sliver of ice. "I've got to figure out a system so I'll be paid by the pound. I ought to get ten times as much for walking that monster as I do for walking Mrs. Farnum's Toodles."

Hank and Jay finished filling the ice chest, and Hank told Jay, "Take ten, kid."

The boys sat on the edge of the dock. Minnows flashed in the sunlit water around the piles. The water boiled as the wake of an outboard swept under the dock. "There's a wise guy," Eddie said. "People are supposed to cut their channel speed to six miles an hour so they won't make a wake."

Jay had recognized the wise guy at the wheel of the outboard as Larry, and sure enough the Great Mal was skimming along behind. "That guy's a good skier," Eddie commented.

Mal was holding the towrope in one hand, shielding his eyes with the other, and Jay knew his brother was checking up on him, finding out whether Jay had told the truth about working at the marina. Jay didn't leap to his feet, eager for his brother to see him, he just lifted a hand and let it fall. "That's the Great Mal," he said.

"Who's the Great Mal?"

"He's my brother, that's all."

Eddie swung around, astonished. "You never said you had a brother! He's really great on those skis. I've seen him before. Gee, it must be great to have an older brother."

"You haven't got any brothers, I take it," Jay said.

"No. If I did I'd have mentioned it. How come you held out on me and didn't tell about yours?"

"You haven't missed anything," Jay said. "You haven't missed a thing, believe you me." He didn't try to keep the bitterness out of his tone.

"You and he don't get along too good?"

"You can say that again!"

They watched the outboard flashing back and forth, just beyond the channel. Even when its course brought Mal across the wakes thrown up by other powerboats he stood upright, arrow straight. "Is he good at other sports?" Eddie asked.

Jay was wishing something would happen to change this conversation. Sports were one interest he and Eddie would never really share. He was about to admit, though, that yes, the Great Mal was indeed a wonderful athlete, when Eddie startled him by shouting, "Hey, do you know what?"

"No, what?"

"Do you know what? Mr. Towner took in an outboard motorboat in trade the other day that's a real wild deal for somebody. It cost five hundred when it was new and he's willing to let it go for three hundred. His business is selling big boats and he doesn't want to bother with the little stuff. Do you want to see it?

With what you make and what I make, maybe we could swing a deal!"

"Sure," Jay said. "Let's go."

As they passed the store Mrs. Shortley darted out to remind Jay he had promised to wash and wax the linoleum for her that morning. "I'll be right back," he told her.

She took his arm. "No, now."

Mr. Towner and George were inside the office and heard all this through the open window. Like everybody else they liked Mrs. Shortley but she really bugged them, because it was her ambition to keep the marina absolutely immaculate. Sometimes Mr. Towner wondered out loud why he had hired such a pesty woman with such a passion for neatness. "Let the kid go," Mr. Towner called. "He'll do your confounded floor for you when he gets a chance." Mrs. Shortley muttered, but she let go of Jay's arm.

"I can't waste much time," he reminded Eddie, as they ran along the south dock, where small boats were moored.

"This is it," Eddie said.

The boat was about fifteen feet long, and painted a rich, dark blue. *Blue Witch* was lettered across the stern. It didn't seem to have any defects; the inside looked clean, and the plastic cushions on the two seats were in good shape. The bow was covered and had doors, behind which stuff could be stored. Jay had to admit, "It looks just great."

"Doesn't it?" Eddie said. "Hey, wouldn't it be some-

thing if we could swing it? How about your dad? Would he be willing to advance you some dough?"

Jay didn't answer right away. He stared at the boat and a great longing swelled in him to do this thing, to buy the *Blue Witch* with Eddie, to be half owner and take her out and go hacking around free as birds on the water, as Mal and his friends did. At the same time he longed intensely to do it on his own. "I hate to ask my dad," he said.

"Why?"

"Oh, reasons," Jay said vaguely. "Family reasons. I'd like to do it on the money I earn myself."

Eddie nodded. "I get your point," he said. "If I can find some more jobs and earn more money I'd like to do the same thing. Do you think we ought to talk to Mr. Towner now? Or do you think we ought to try first to get some other kids to put dough in it and go shares with us?"

"I think it would be better if just the two of us could swing it," Jay said. He didn't want to share the boat and he didn't want any other boys to come barging into his and Eddie's friendship.

"Okay. Let's talk to Mr. Towner."

They started off, turning to look back to see if the boat was all they thought it was. She really had an air. She had nice, sporty lines, and that dark blue color was beautiful. "Come on!" Jay urged, breaking into a run.

"What's the hurry?"

"We'd better get there quick, before some other guys get the same idea," Jay said.

8

THEY WERE PANTING when they burst into the store.
Mr. Towner led them into his office and told them to
sit down and get their breath back.

On his desk rested a beautiful chocolate cake. Mrs.
Shortley was probably the finest cook in the world. She
lived alone, and had adopted the marina gang as her
family, and often brought fresh-baked cookies or a pie
or a cake when she came to work.

The boys accepted pieces on paper plates. "Don't
drop any crumbs or that woman will tack my hide to
the wall," the boss warned. "Now, what's on your
minds?"

He heard them out, how they wanted to buy the blue
boat but were short of actual cash. When it came down
to cold figures, Jay admitted he had only thirty-one dol-

lars to put in. Eddie had saved a little over twenty dollars out of his dog-walking business. "Hmmm," the boss mused. "We'll round it off at fifty dollars for the down payment."

"That's not much, is it?" Jay asked.

"It's not too good, but it's not too bad either," Mr. Towner told them. "You're both working, that's in your favor. If you keep your noses clean and don't fool around, probably both of you can look forward to a steady income for the rest of the summer. If you each put in twenty dollars a week you'll own the boat free and clear by Labor Day."

"Could we use it, even though you own more of it than we do?" Eddie asked.

"Yes, of course. It's no good to me, just sitting at the dock. How about a motor? What do you plan to do about that?"

"We haven't any plans in mind," Eddie admitted.

"I'll speak to Bo," Mr. Towner said. "He may have some beat-up old outboard he'll let you have cheap."

They tried to thank him, but he just waved his cigar at them and turned his back.

Noon had come and it was time for Jay to quit. He was just as glad because the day had come off very hot. The thermometer outside the shop door registered ninety. Eddie said, "Hey, I've got a brilliant idea, let's get a sandwich at the restaurant and go swimming."

"Okay," Jay agreed. His heart sank, though, down to his sneakers. Eddie was going to find out he couldn't swim. Just the same, he had to agree. Having a friend

81

was so important to him he had to go along with anything Eddie suggested.

They started up the steps to the restaurant, and then Eddie paused. "We can't spend money on food," he said. "We've got to save every cent. We'd better eat at home, where the food's free."

"All right," Jay said. "I'll go home and eat and meet you back here."

"You live way over at the Point?"

"That's right, but it won't take me long."

"I've got a better idea," Eddie announced. "We'll eat on my boat. My mother will fix something."

Jay hesitated. He was excited by the suggestion of having lunch on the Princes' boat. The *Sara S.* was a new, forty-foot beauty, and he thought Eddie's father must be a very successful doctor to own such a fine boat. Mrs. Prince lived aboard it, using it as a summer home, and the doctor came for the weekends.

Even more than he wanted to visit Eddie's boat, though, Jay wanted to offer the hospitality of his own home. This would be a new thing for him, to bring a guest. What would happen if Mal was home? Nervousness made Jay hesitate, but he got up his courage. "No, you come home with me," he said. "My mother or Emma will make us some sandwiches."

"Okay," Eddie agreed. "Do you think I'd better clean up and put on another shirt?"

"No. We can wash when we get there. Your shirt's all right."

They took it easy, because the road shimmered,

throwing heat in their faces. Eddie chattered on, saying they should tackle Bo that afternoon to find out if he had an old motor he could sell them. Jay interrupted. "If my brother's home for lunch, would you just as soon not mention the boat?" he asked. "I'm not ready yet to break the news to my folks."

"Enough said," Eddie agreed. "Mum's the word."

Major heard their voices as they came up the drive, and barked and whined. Jay got down on his knees to hug him and Major explored Jay's ears with his tongue, crying with joy. "That dog's really crazy about you," Eddie said, sounding envious.

Jay untied the rope and the three entered the kitchen. "Anybody home?" Jay called. He was almost praying that Mal wouldn't answer. What Jay didn't need today was to have Mal slouching around, either acting like a big shot or else getting nosy and asking a lot of questions.

No, Mal didn't answer. Emma did, and she didn't sound too happy. She came out of the pantry with a bucket in her hand. Apparently she had been scrubbing. "Where's Mom?" Jay asked nervously.

"She went to a lunch party with some of her lady-friends."

Emma eyed Major and Jay knew what was coming next — she was going to let fly at him because he'd brought his dog into her clean house. He got the jump on her. "Emma, I'd like you to meet my friend, Eddie Prince," he said. "Eddie, this is Mrs. Emma Hodge. She's a real great cook!"

"How do you do, Mrs. Hodge," Eddie said politely.

"Emma, do you mind if we make some sandwiches, if we clean up afterward?" Jay asked.

She set her pail in the sink and dried her hands. "Sit down," she ordered. "I'll feed you. Whenever I get two polite young-uns to feed, I want to make the most of it. That brother of yours just left, Jay, and he didn't ask, much less say 'Please.' He ransacked the place and broke a jar of pickles, and left the mess for me to clean up. He didn't find the good stuff, though!"

Jay showed Eddie where the bathroom was, and they washed. When they returned to the kitchen they found that Emma had set out a feast, peanut butter sandwiches, cold fried chicken, iced tea, and cookies.

Major cowered under the table. Jay didn't blame him, for Emma's voice was loud and harsh, and Major didn't know her bark was worse than her bite. Emma sat at the table with a cup of tea. She was so near Major trembled even worse as he pressed against Jay.

She raised the red-checked cloth and looked at him. "Hmmmph!" she snorted. "He's got no reason to be so scared of me. Major, that's a mighty impressive name for such an insignificant dog!"

They finished eating and carried their dishes to the sink, and Eddie said, "Thank you for the nice lunch, Mrs. Hodge."

"Yes, thanks a lot," Jay echoed.

"You can come anytime," Emma told Eddie. "I can always whip up an extra sandwich."

Jay tied Major's rope and they set off. Jay was

ashamed of his dog's old chain collar and his piece of clothesline. Boat or no boat, he intended to spend some of his hard-earned money and buy Major a good collar and leash, the next time he got paid.

He told Eddie about Emma's bark being worse than her bite, and Eddie nodded. "That's the way I had her figured," he said. "The next time, you'll have to come to my boat and eat. My mom won't put out a spread like that, though, on such short notice."

They by-passed the marina's tiled swimming pool. The little kids and their mothers monopolized it in the afternoons. Besides, Mr. Towner charged fifty cents for using it. The pebbly crescent of beach beyond the work area and the boat lift was plenty good enough for swimming.

Roy Atkins was there before them. Jay knew him by sight, and knew he was a local boy who lived all year round on the island. Judging by his size, Jay thought he must be thirteen, or even fourteen. Jay couldn't tell, by the way Roy and Eddie greeted each other, whether they were just acquaintances or were real friends.

"I'll beat you two out to that clump of rocks," Roy said. He rushed into the water and dived under. Eddie splashed after him.

The moment of truth had come for Jay. He couldn't follow, for he would have sunk like a stone and drowned. Walking on his hands and making believe he was swimming wouldn't work, either. The boys would see immediately that he was pulling a kid trick.

He stood at the edge, feeling left out and completely miserable. All his new self-confidence was gone. He was a loner again, right back where he started before he got the job at the marina and began to be somebody.

"Come on," Eddie urged.

Jay took refuge in a lie. "I can't," he called back. "I've got a cramp in my leg."

"You haven't got a cramp, you haven't even been in the water yet!" Roy yelled.

Jay didn't answer. He wasn't much good at solving his own problems; usually, he just walked away from them. Now all he wanted to do was to put on his sneakers and untie his dog and leave.

If he did that, though, he would be walking away from his friendship with Eddie, and their plan to buy the boat and all that. He might even have to give up his job at the marina. How could he show his face there again, when all the boys knew he was just a joke to be laughed at?

He was still standing there, miserably trying to make up his mind what to do, when Eddie swam back to shore. Roy had stretched out on the rocks to sun himself. "What's the matter?" Eddie asked.

Jay thought fast. What lie would cover this situation? Saying he had a bum heart, something like that? Saying his doctor wouldn't let him go swimming?

All this flashed through Jay's mind, but what came out was the truth. "Do you want to know something really dumb?" he said with a shaky laugh. "I don't know how to swim."

9

"You're kidding," Eddie said. Jay shook his head.

He could tell by the way Eddie stared at him that Eddie was really disillusioned. A twelve-year-old boy who couldn't take care of himself in the water — that was an unheard of thing. Jay fully expected Eddie to say, "So long, kid, see you around," and then rejoin Roy on the rocks.

Eddie picked up a stone and skipped it, and he was an expert; it took four skips before it sank. "Well," he said, "I sure picked myself a fine partner for that boat deal. You'll have to learn, that's all."

"Maybe I could get George or Hank to teach me."

"Yeah, and have it get all around the marina that you don't know how to swim? How about your brother, why didn't he ever teach you?"

"If I was drowning and going down for the third time, I wouldn't ask him," Jay said.

"You really hate him."

"You can say that again."

"Why?"

Jay didn't answer. What was the point of going back over the years and hauling up all the things Mal had ever done to cut a younger brother down to size?

Eddie waited, and finally he said, "You're really a mixed-up kid, do you know that, Jay? It looks like I'm elected to teach you how to swim. Now you'd better stick with that story about having a cramp." He pulled Jay down on the sand and began vigorously rubbing the calf of Jay's leg.

He put on such a good act Roy didn't guess the truth. He joined them and they sprawled on the sand, watching the boats passing in the channel, talking idly. Roy mentioned he had heard that a couple of kids were buying the *Blue Witch,* and that he'd had his eye on the boat because it was a great buy.

"Yeah," Eddie said nonchalantly, "that's us."

"You're kidding," Roy said.

"No, we've got a deal on, with Mr. Towner."

"No kidding?"

"No kidding."

"You mean your folks are buying it for you. I bet your folks and Jay's are really loaded."

"No, we're earning the money."

"Say!" Roy exclaimed. "If that's the case, how about taking me in, too? I've got sort of a business, mowing lawns. I could put in a third. We could own it three ways."

Eddie turned to Jay. Jay didn't speak. "I don't know," Eddie said vaguely. "Suppose we let you know, Roy. Well, I guess I'd better mosey down to the dock and let my mother know I'm still alive. She hasn't seen me since I left this morning."

Jay ran all the way home; hot as it was, he felt like running. He had the feeling he needed to escape from a new set of problems. What if Eddie thought it over and decided he didn't care to be best friends with a dopey kid who was so dumb he had never learned to swim, who didn't know anything about sports and all the other stuff boys were supposed to know?

What if Eddie decided he wanted to take Roy into partnership? That could end up with Roy squeezing Jay out of the *Blue Witch* deal. It was an easy thing to do, because not once in his whole life had Jay ever stood up and fought for anything he wanted.

Major ran at his side. Looking down at him Jay thought, maybe he is sort of an insignificant dog to have such a big name. Then, when Jay slowed to get his breath, Major got in front of him and put his front paws on Jay's chest, asking to be petted.

He was a tall dog, so their faces weren't a foot apart. What Jay saw in his dog's eyes gave him a great feeling. In the gold-flecked depths he saw fear and love mixed up together, and a look of hope, as though Major was beginning to believe he had really found somebody he could belong to.

The same thing went for Jay, in spades. He too had found somebody he dared belong to, his dog. "You don't have to sweat it, Major," he said, rubbing the soft brown ears. "You and I are going to stick together."

Maybe it was running in the sun on such a hot afternoon that did it, but a blinding headache struck Jay as he neared his house. He could hardly see when he entered the kitchen. "Is that you, Jay?" his mother called from the living room.

"It's me," he croaked.

"Where have you been all day?"

He didn't answer, and she came to find him. "You're white as a sheet," she said.

He told her about the headache, and she gave him aspirin and made him lie on the sofa with a cool cloth over his eyes, and brought him a tall glass of pineapple juice. Major curled down next to the sofa.

Jay must have slept, because the shadows were long when he took off the cloth. His headache was better. Mal was hunched over the table, whistling softly between his teeth, absorbed in something. Jay lay and watched for a while, and finally his curiosity got the better of him and he went to look over his brother's shoulder.

Mal had the plastic parts of a toy automobile in front of him, and was trying to stick them together with airplane glue. He glanced up. "Hi, kid," he said. "Feel any better? Mom was scared, she thought you might have sunstroke or something."

"No, I'm all right," Jay said.

It was a long, long time since they had held a friendly conversation like this. "You know about this stuff," Mal went on. "You've made these models. What's this thing?"

"It looks like the front bumper."

"What are these, then?"

"They're the wheel assembly."

Mal didn't invite him but Jay sat down anyway, and began fiddling with the pieces. Soon he was handing Mal parts and Mal was sticking them, and the car took shape. Mrs. Sharp came in and found them that way, working together, and she didn't say anything but she looked very pleased. Jay guessed it was a treat to her to find them doing something besides snarling and getting ready to leap at each other's throats.

When the car was finished Mal set it on a tall shelf to dry, and it looked fine, a model of an antique Pierce Arrow, in red and gold. "Hey, that's pretty good. Hey, you're not so stupid, brother," Mal said.

Jay gave him a sort of a grin. "How come you're wasting an afternoon on a kid project like this?" he asked.

"I saw it in a store and I had a buck, so I bought it."

They didn't fight at dinner, either. Mal didn't yell at Jay once. A buddy of Mal's came after dinner and they went off in his buddy's car to hack around, but Mal came home early. Jay had gone to his room and he heard his brother come whistling up the stairs.

Jay had always closed his bedroom door at night because he liked to be alone, but tonight he left it open, knowing his dog would come seeking him. Major did. He jumped off the bed, though, and crawled under it when Mrs. Sharp came in.

She asked Jay how he felt. Then she said, "Mal was worried about you this afternoon, too. It was his idea that he should work on his model in the living room, so he could keep an eye on you."

What was Jay supposed to say? "That's great, so now Mal and I will bury the hatchet and be bosom buddies?" Maybe that was what he should have have said but he didn't. He just didn't give any answer.

She sighed, and stood up. "Your brother does love you, and deep down you love him, too, darling. I wish you'd find that out soon, before it's too late," she said, and went away.

Jay had failed her, he knew that. His habit of keeping a sullen silence was too strong.

He could hear his brother moving around in the next room. Should he ask Mal to teach him to swim? His stock would go up with Eddie, he knew, if he could tell Eddie he didn't have to bother to teach him, because Jay's own brother was doing it.

Jay was still wondering the next morning whether he could get up the nerve to ask for Mal's help. He did his work at the marina and got paid, and he and Eddie had a conference with Mr. Towner and handed over the down payment on the boat. Nothing was said by Eddie about taking Roy into partnership.

They sponged their boat out, and found it leaked a little, but not enough to worry about. Jay had noticed how some of the boat people made bailers for their dinghies. He rummaged in Mrs. Shortley's supply closet and found a plastic bleach bottle which was almost empty. He poured its contents into another which was almost full. He cut the bottom half off with scissors, and shaped the upper half, which had a handle. It made a scoop that was a perfect bailer.

Eddie thought this was the neatest trick of the week and said so. Jay made light of it, but Eddie's praise was music in his ears. Every time he had a small success he felt a little surer of himself, a bit more self-confident.

"How about going swimming?" Eddie asked.

"Sure. Okay, I guess," Jay told him.

Eddie was naturally tactful and didn't suggest they go to the beach near the marina. They kept their sneakers on and made their way along the large boulders, covered with seaweed, which lined the shore. When they were out of sight of any observers Eddie said, "This place will do."

He bent over, untying his sneakers. "What's your hang-up?" he asked.

"What do you mean?"

"How come you never learned to swim? You spend every summer here, near the water. So how come?"

Jay felt a sudden, burning desire to confide in Eddie, to pour out the whole story of how hating his brother was screwing up his life. He almost did. "My brother's a real hot-shot swimmer," he began. Then he stopped. "I don't know," he said, laughing in a silly way. "I guess I'm just naturally stupid."

"Yeah, you're stupid," Eddie said. "Stupid enough to get yourself a job at the marina that every other kid would give his eyeteeth for. Come on." He walked into the water.

"Are you going to hang on to me?" Jay asked.

"Maybe so, maybe not."

"I'll go under. My feet will drag me down."

"Sure you'll go under," Eddie said. "So what? You'll come up again. Just hold your breath."

"I can't."

"Yes, you can. If you've got a choice between drowning and holding your breath, then you'll hold your breath."

Jay waded out. "Get over on your belly," Eddie ordered. Eddie took hold of the waistband of Jay's swimming trunks. Jay kicked his feet, making wild sweeps with his arms in imitation of a crawl stroke. He was puffing and spraying water all over the place when he felt Eddie's grasp loosen. He promptly sank.

Eddie reached down and fished him up. Jay stood coughing and sputtering, salt water acrid in his throat. "You dumb cluck, you didn't hold your breath," Eddie said crossly. "We'll try again. Keep kicking and moving your arms."

Twice more Jay went down. The last time, though, he held his breath. Eddie didn't fish him up, he rose by himself to the surface. The next time they tried, Jay

94

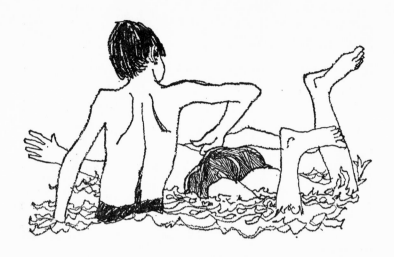

just kept moving his legs when he felt Eddie's grasp
loosen. He thrashed with his arms and he actually
swam a little way.

He looked back and saw that Eddie was several feet
away and then he panicked, stopped moving, and sank
to the bottom. Somehow, though, he remembered not
to breathe. His head broke through the surface and he
stood up, so far from shore only his head was above the
water.

Eddie joined him. "There," he said, "that's all there
is to it. Now you can swim. I'll sit on a rock and you
keep trying. Tomorrow I'll show you a proper kick
and a real crawl stroke, and I'll show you how to float.
But you can't drown now. Anybody who can swim ten
feet can swim a hundred feet."

Jay kept practicing. Sometimes when he looked up
Eddie was watching, and sometimes Eddie was gazing

out to sea. When at last Jay stumbled to the shore, he was exhausted. He was sick at his stomach because he had swallowed salt water, but he felt calm inside, at peace with the world.

They used their T-shirts to wipe themselves dry, and started back to the marina. "Thanks, Eddie," Jay croaked.

This was on a Friday. Jay's parents had a dinner engagement that evening, and Mal and Jay ate from trays in front of the TV. Emma went home after she had washed the dishes, and soon after Mal went off with one of his pals.

It was still light, for the sun didn't drop into the western sea until almost eight-thirty. Jay took his dog for a long walk along the beach. He looked at the water and asked himself, Do I dare? and answered himself, Yes, I dare. He still had on his swim trunks under his regular pants. He tied Major's rope to a stone and waded in.

There wasn't a soul in sight, nobody to rescue him if he started to drown, but he didn't plan to drown. He got over on his belly and did his imitation of a swim stroke and it worked. His longest swim was about twenty feet. It took him out of his depth, and when he put his feet down there was nothing there. He had a vision of sinking into the green depths and lying there forever, but just then he heard Major's terrified howl. He doggedly kept his feet and arms going, moving toward the shore, and soon his toes scraped gravel.

Major leaped at him as he staggered up the beach,

and licked the salt off his face. Together they walked along the shingle to the Point. Jay felt suddenly ten feet tall. His fear of the water was gone. He knew the sea could never drown him now.

10

Maybe he was feeling his oats and maybe he acted cocky that following week. Anyway, Mal gave him some funny looks the next Friday afternoon when they were hanging around, waiting to go with their mother to the train.

She planned to meet her husband with the news that he was taking the family out to dinner and to a movie. They all liked Chinese food, and the picture at the drive-in was a good one.

Mr. Sharp was in a fine mood because he had had a successful week and had won an important case, so he cheerfully fell in with her plan. He gave them a blow-by-blow account of the case while he drove to the shopping center and parked the car near the Chinese restaurant.

They all chose different dishes, planning to share them. While they waited, Mr. Sharp inquired, "And what kind of a week did my ever-lovin' family have?"

"Nothing much happened, but it was a nice week," his wife told him.

Mal evidently decided that he ought to make hay while the sun shone, since his father was in such a good mood. "Dad, the summer's going fast, do you know that?" he asked.

"What do you have in mind, son?"

"What I mean is, if we're going to get a boat we ought to do it now, so we'd get some use of it," Mal said.

"So we're back on the subject of boats."

"Yep, we're back on that subject," Mal said with a grin. "I've been looking over the field, pretty thoroughly, and I've been hoping you'd go tomorrow and look at some. There are three places in the area that sell new boats, and that used boat I told you about a while back is still for sale."

"How do you feel about it, Jay?" Mr. Sharp asked. "If we go into such a project you boys will have to understand that it's a joint venture. In the past you haven't done too well, sharing things. I don't want to put money into a boat and then find out it's just a bone of contention between you two. Your mother's peaceful summer would be wrecked, and so would my weekends."

The waiter came, bringing a heavy tray. He set the dishes on the table, and while the family was busy passing them, piling their plates, Jay had a chance to think. He was hoping the subject would be dropped, because he was very sure that if he broke his news he would start new trouble with Mal.

Mr. Sharp went back to it, though. "How about it, Jay?" he asked.

Jay hesitated. Then he said, "I guess you'll have to count me out, Dad. I've already got a half interest in a boat."

They all looked at him. "What are you talking about?" Mal demanded.

"Yes, what do you mean, son?" his father asked. "Do you know about this, Mary?"

"I haven't the faintest idea what Jay's been up to," Mrs. Sharp said. "Now let's eat our dinner before it gets cold."

Mal and Mr. Sharp were still waiting for Jay to explain. "I'm going shares on a boat with a friend of mine, Eddie Prince," Jay told them. "It's an outboard, a sixteen-footer. Somebody turned it in on a new one, and Mr. Towner gave us a good price. Bo's fixing us up with a motor."

"And who is Bo?"

"Bo Brown. He's boss of the repair department at the marina."

If looks could have killed, Jay would have dropped dead because of the one Mal gave him across the table. It wasn't Jay's fault he had queered Mal's pitch for a new boat, but that was the result. Jay squirmed, and the chop suey he was eating was hard to swallow. He knew he would have to contend with Mal's wrath later, when they were alone.

Mr. Sharp asked more questions, about how Jay planned to meet the payments and what condition the boat was in, and whether Jay knew there were safety regulations to meet in owning a boat. Finally the subject was dropped. They finished dinner and went to the drive-in and sat in the car and watched the spy movie.

Mr. Sharp brought the matter up again, after they reached home. "Jay, the question of insurance on your boat bothers me," he said. "Do you want me to talk to Mr. Towner, and perhaps see the father of your friend, what's his name, Eddie?"

"Sure, Dad, that will be great," Jay said. "Maybe Mom would like to come, too, and see where I work and see the boat and all."

"We'll go tomorrow morning," Mr. Sharp told him.

An evening spent so pleasantly hadn't cooled Mal's anger. Jay discovered that when he went up to bed and found Mal waiting in his room. Major was waiting, too, and just as Jay walked in Major crawled under the bed.

Seeing that the dog was afraid of him seemed to make Mal even angrier. "Anybody'd think I hit that mutt," he said. "Well, I didn't. That's a great dog you've got. You're having a great summer, little brother, you're getting everything your own way. You bring home a mangy hound that's afraid of its own shadow and everybody thinks that's wonderful — darling Jay has his own sweet little dog. Now you put on an act, the big shot buying his own boat. You and I know you're not going to pay for it out of the few bucks you make, doing odd jobs at that great marina! You're going to come whining to Dad for help."

Jay longed to say, "Shut your face!" The habit of being afraid of his brother was too strong. "No, I won't," he said.

"You were trying to make me look cheap."

"No, I wasn't."

The two had scuffled many times, and every time Jay had gotten the worst of it. He often wished that his eyes were bad, so he could wear glasses and have an excuse for not fighting. Only once, though, had Mal actually hauled off and hit him. The look on Mal's face now said that was exactly what he longed to do.

Jay was hoping against hope that his parents would appear and break up the fight before it started. He jerked the bed out and scrambled behind it. Try as he might, he couldn't keep the quaver out of his voice. "Please, Mal," he begged.

Mal lunged across the bed. A low growl came from under it, then a snarl. Mal yelled, and all of a sudden he was groveling on the floor with Major's teeth sunk in his ankle. He cuffed at the dog's head but Major shut his eyes and hung on. Mal succeeded in getting his other leg free and kicking the dog off, and Major crawled under the bed again but continued to growl.

"What's going on up there?" Mr. Sharp called up the stairs.

102

"Nothing, Dad. It's okay," Mal called back.

Jay emerged from behind the bed. Mal pulled down his sock to look. The teeth marks showed, but the skin wasn't broken.

Mal got to his feet. "You make me sick," he said. "You got that dog so he could do your fighting for you. You never stand and fight. Just once, why can't you take a poke at me? You always cry. You get your way because you blubber like a baby."

Mal went to the door. "You make me so sick, I wish I didn't have a brother," he said, and slammed the door.

Jay didn't wash or even brush his teeth. He got into bed, but sleep wouldn't come. When he closed his eyes he saw his brother's face, and the cold dislike on it. When had Mal ever treated him kindly, like a real older brother? Why should he have to hit Mal, to prove he wasn't afraid?

What was so great about fighting, anyhow? he wondered. It took more brains to get and hold a job than it did to stand up for your rights by fighting. That was what was the matter with the whole world — everybody thought they had to fight to prove something. To prove what?

Jay spent a miserable hour, trying to justify himself. Finally, worn out by thinking, he fell asleep.

All was calm on the surface when he went down to breakfast the next morning. His parents didn't seem to know there had been a quarrel. Mal limped, but he didn't mention that Major had attacked him.

Mrs. Sharp suggested that Mal might like to come with them to the marina, to see where Jay worked and to see the boat. "No, thanks," Mal said shortly.

Jay had so little self-confidence he worried about the kind of reception his mother and father would receive at the marina, but he could have saved himself that worry. His friends gave them a hearty welcome, as though they were important just because they were Jay's parents.

When Jay led them into the store and said, "Boss, these are my folks," Mr. Towner ushered them into his private office and cleared chairs for them. The word got around and George Thawless dropped in to meet them, and Hank stopped by to say hello. Mrs. Shortley produced a box of her famous brownies, and put her arm around Jay's shoulders and really poured it on, telling how important he was around the place.

"We think a lot of your boy, Mrs. Sharp," Mr. Towner agreed. "He keeps himself busy, and willingly does whatever is asked of him. He earns his pay, don't worry about that."

"He's a cheery little soul," Mrs. Shortley added. "He has a smile for everybody."

Jay glanced up and saw the baffled expressions on his parents' faces. At home Jay moved silently around and very rarely volunteered a remark, and he guessed he didn't smile very often.

Mr. Towner and Mr. Sharp discussed insurance, and Mr. Towner showed Jay's father the policy he recommended, which would cover the boys in case they hit anybody in the water, or did any other type of damage.

When the men had finished, Jay set out with his parents to call on Dr. and Mrs. Prince. Eddie came running up the dock to meet them. "Dad and Mom, this is my best friend, Eddie Prince," Jay announced.

This was another first. Today was the first time grownups had ever praised him to his parents, telling how cheerful and helpful he was. Today was also the first time he had ever presented a boy to his folks and been able to say, "This is my best friend."

They all walked along the dock together while Jay pointed out the dockhouse, which he kept tidy, the ice chest where he delivered the ice, the gas and diesel pumps. He told how he occasionally serviced boats and managed the gas dock.

His luck was really in, today. Just then a forty-two-foot yacht glided up, a man tossed the bow line, and Jay caught it. "Gas or diesel?" he asked. The man said his engines took diesel oil, and Jay, with Eddie's help, walked the boat along the dock to the diesel pump. This looked like a harder trick than it was, really, for two boys could easily move a heavy boat along from post to post, but Jay's father looked very impressed. Jay tied the line with his best square knot. The man called out, "Thanks, kids," and Jay answered with a careless flip of his hand indicating it was nothing, that he and Eddie were just as capable of tying up an ocean liner if one came up the channel.

Mrs. Prince was aboard the *Sara S.* Jay had eaten

lunch twice there, so he and Eddie's mother were friends. She invited them all aboard, explaining that she was sorry her husband wasn't around to meet them. Jay's mother exclaimed what a beautiful boat the *Sara S.* was, and Mrs. Prince asked, "Would you like to see it?" The two women went below to explore.

When they came back up they were chattering, and it was easy to see that they liked each other. Mrs. Sharp invited Eddie's parents to come the next day, for a swim and a cold drink.

It was time to go. Jay was in a happy daze because everything had worked out very well. Mr. Towner stuck his head out of his office window to call, "See you Monday morning, Jay."

Mr. Sharp rumpled Jay's hair as they were getting into the car. "It looks to me like you've got it made, son," he said.

11

J AY WORKED HARD all Monday morning, doing his jobs thoroughly because he felt very grateful to the marina people for being so nice when he brought his folks to visit. He was in such a state of excitement, though, the morning hours just dragged. This was the great day when he and Eddie were to take their boat out for the first time.

He assumed that Eddie knew all about outboard motors, and Eddie assumed the same thing about him. Neither thought to ask the other if he knew how to run one.

They met at one o'clock. Both had brought sandwiches, and they stopped to buy cans of soda from the soda machine. They acted like adventurers, setting out on a great expedition. They planned to explore Three Penny Island, a deserted, grass-covered piece of land that flanked the channel at the mouth of the river.

Bo hailed them from the door of his shop. "Hey, you two! I don't suppose you thought about gas." They admitted he was right, and he handed them a full can. "The can's free, but you owe me seventy cents for the gas," he told them. They fished in their pockets, but they couldn't get up that amount. Bo agreed they could owe it until the next day.

Roy Atkins was lounging on the small-boat dock when they arrived. He seemed to know that today they were taking possession. Maybe he was still sore because they had refused to include him in. "Now we'll see how the great boat owners operate," he announced, and leaned on a pile to watch.

Jay still expected Eddie to take command. They filled the gas tank. Eddie waited. "Go ahead, turn her over," he ordered. Then they looked at each other and laughed, realizing that neither knew what to do. "We'll have to ask Bo to come down and show us," Eddie said. "I'll go get him."

"Hold on," Roy ordered, with a happier look on his wide face. "If you ignoramuses don't even know how to start it, I'll show you." He jumped aboard.

Jay felt like clobbering him, and Eddie's scowl showed he felt the same, because of the arrogant way Roy went about it. He showed them how to adjust the choke, how to wind the starting rope and jerk it until the motor sputtered, and then how to throttle it down.

109

The motor let out a hearty blast, which was music in their ears. They were as nervous and clumsy as the worst kind of landlubbers. Jay almost fell overboard when he hauled in the bow line to untie it.

Eddie perched on the stern seat, his hand on the tiller. "Go ahead," Roy called. "Give it the gas."

Eddie did so and the motor roared, but the boat didn't move. Roy danced up and down on the dock. "You dopes, you didn't untie the stern line!" he howled gleefully.

Jay fell all over Eddie to get to it. Eddie gave her the gun, the *Blue Witch* shot forward, and Jay landed in a

heap in the bottom. He picked himself up and sub-
sided on a seat.

Roy was racing up the dock. "He looks like Paul Re-
vere, spreading the news that we made fools of our-
selves," Jay told Eddie.

Eddie didn't answer because he was having troubles.
A bellow, "Watch it!" made him veer just in time out
of the path of a boat backing into its slip.

"Slow it down," Jay suggested.

"How?" Eddie demanded. "If you're the great expert suppose you sit back here!"

By now they had reached the middle of the channel.

Eddie was too busy fumbling with the motor, trying to find the gadget that would cut the speed, to watch where he was going. Jay stood up and had a moment of sheer panic as the boat rocked wildly, threatening to toss him into deep water. Then the *Blue Witch* lurched and threw him into the stern seat beside Eddie. He grabbed the tiller.

A sailboat was bearing down on them, tacking across the channel, and the man at her wheel frantically waved his arms, a look of horror on his face. Jay threw the tiller over hard and the *Blue Witch* sheered off, but the boats scraped sides. Jay looked up and the sailboat's skipper looked down, and neither said a word.

By now the *Blue Witch* had crossed the channel and they were out of the traffic. At last Eddie found the throttle, and eased it back. The motor coughed and almost died, then held at a steady hum. "Here, you don't need me, you steer it," Jay said, getting ready to move.

"No, stay here," Eddie ordered. "It takes two to manage this monster."

Jay chuckled, and Eddie began to giggle, and they laughed together hysterically, mostly because they were so relieved to have survived their first sea trip so far. When they stopped they heard a faint, "Hey! Jay, Eddie!"

The gas dock of the marina was a quarter-mile away now, but they could make out Roy, George, Hank, and Mrs. Prince shading their eyes, watching. George yelled something but they couldn't make out the words, so they waved back to tell him all was well with them now.

The water was glassy flat as they glided along at slow speed. "This is a bit of all right," Eddie said happily.

Jay glanced over the side, and saw why the water was so calm. The bottom was only two feet down. He watched a blue crab scuttle off sidewise. The eelgrass waved lazily, and it seemed to Jay it was very thick. "Hey, I don't think this is such a great place to be," he began.

With that the motor gave a sick cough and died. The silence was practically deafening. "I guess that's what George was yelling, to warn us about the eelgrass," Jay mentioned.

They both knelt on the stern seat. The slimy reeds had wrapped around the propeller and it looked hopelessly tangled. "Ugh," Eddie said. "Who's going over the side to clear away that mess?"

Jay hesitated. "Was your father ever in the army?" Eddie asked.

"Yes," Jay said. "Why?"

"I bet he learned the same thing my dad did, never to volunteer. Here, I've got a nickel. Heads, you go over, tails, I do."

The coin flashed and Eddie caught it. "Heads," he said.

Jay took off his sneakers, rolled up his dungarees, and eased over the side. He imagined all sorts of slippery creatures, crawling in the mud, as his feet hit the cold bottom. He sank over his ankles, and shuddered. He made his way to the stern, bent down, and began pulling away the grass, working under water.

Eddie found a rusty screwdriver under the bow cover, and that made the tangle easier to loosen. Eddie, sitting high and dry in the boat, watched Jay struggle and continued to give advice. Finally Jay lost patience. "Look, if you can do any better, be my guest!" he snapped. "Come on in, the water's fine."

Right away he was sorry. He couldn't afford to quarrel with Eddie. Where would he ever find another friend like him? He opened his mouth to apologize.

Eddie did it first. "Don't mind me," he said. "I always like to give away advice, on account of it's free. You're doing a great job."

They were so absorbed they didn't notice another boat until it drifted alongside. When Jay finally glanced up, there was Mal.

Larry was with him. "Is this the boat you kids bought?" Larry asked. "It's not a bad-looking tub."

His brother was the last person in the world Jay wanted to see at that particular moment. He was handing Mal the chance of a lifetime, to make a crack that would really cut him down to size. "Hi," Jay muttered.

He grudgingly did the honors, "Eddie, this is my brother, Mal. The other guy's Larry."

The older boys watched his struggles for a while. Finally Mal said, "It's your own fault, getting into the eelgrass."

"Yeah," Eddie said. "This is our maiden voyage,
you might say. We didn't look where we were going."

"Do you want any help, Squirt?" Mal asked Jay.

Jay kept his head down, working away at the tangle.
He ought to say, "No, we don't need any help from
you," or else, more politely, "No, thanks just the
same." Instead the words came out differently. "Yes, I
could sure use some help. This is a real mess."

Larry started to take off his sneakers but Mal said,
"I'll do it. It's my brother who got himself into this
snafu." He kicked off his shoes, rolled up his pant legs,
and joined Jay in the mud.

Jay handed him the screwdriver. Larry showed Eddie how to release the catch and tip the motor up, so the brothers didn't have to work under water. The tangled grass loosened and floated away. The job was done.

Jay was so confused he didn't know what to think. Why had Mal passed up such a golden opportunity to make him look like a fool?

"Look, you guys," Eddie was saying, "maybe you'll show us how to choke the motor and then throttle it down. We either go about sixty miles an hour or we don't go at all."

Mal climbed into the boat, then turned to give Jay a helping hand. "Hey!" Eddie exclaimed, "you two stink!"

He was right, the mud did have a real ripe smell. Mal and Jay splashed their feet and washed off the mud.

Larry was studying the motor. "How much did you pay for the outboard?" he asked.

"Thirty-five dollars," Eddie told him.

"You got a bargain. You kids must really rate with that marina owner," Larry said.

Mal carefully explained how an outboard motor worked. He asked where Jay and Eddie planned to go and they said Three Penny Island. He climbed over into Larry's boat and said with a grin, "Lots of luck, you'll need it." Larry gave his motor the gun and zoomed off, Eddie and Jay yelling after them, "Thanks!"

Jay's mind was still in a whirl. How come? he wondered. Mal had every right to resent the *Blue Witch*. He'd lost his chance to get a boat when the news came out that Jay was working to earn his.

Eddie took the tiller and got back into the channel without picking up more weeds than the propeller could handle. He brought the *Blue Witch* very nicely up the shingle beach of Three Penny. Jay jumped out, pulled her high, and tied the line to a big rock so the outgoing tide wouldn't carry her away.

By now they were starved, and so they sat down on the sand and ate their sandwiches and drank their soda.

"Let's bring Major over here," Jay suggested. "We have to find out if he's a good boat dog or if he gets seasick."

Eddie wasn't listening. "Your brother seems like a good egg," he said. "Do you know, for the life of me I can't figure out why you hate him. So he called you 'Squirt,' so what? Calling names like that doesn't mean anything. Boy! If you knew what it was like to be the only kid in a family, you'd think it was great to have a brother, even if you did fight."

What could Jay say? He couldn't rake up all the mean, belittling things Mal had done to him since the year one, since the day he was born. He couldn't say, "My brother was just putting on an act, making like a good guy."

He just wasn't sure the last was the truth. He was silent, gazing out over the water but not really seeing anything. A terrible doubt had hold of him.

He remembered something his father had said to him once. "Jay, you think Mal ought to be perfect," he had said. "Are you sure you're perfect, son? You have to take Mal the way he is. You have to take the world the way it is, with all its faults."

Eddie broke in on his thoughts. "Hey, what's the matter with you?"

"Nothing," Jay said. He jumped up and stuffed the wax paper from his sandwich in his pocket. "Come on, let's explore."

There wasn't much to see. They had heard that, once, somebody had built a shack on the island, but it had been swept away by a hurricane. They found the rocks of the foundation. They considered whether someday, when they grew up and got jobs, they might buy Three Penny and build houses on it. Then they decided that the island was so low no sea wall would keep out a really high tide.

They circled it, picking up junk — a lobster-pot buoy, sea-scoured stones, empty shells of tiny crabs tangled in dry seaweed. Then they climbed into their boat and set a course upriver.

Roy was waiting at the floating dock to catch the bow line, and he grinned in an "I-told-you-so" sort of way. George wasn't grinning, he was scowling, when they ran into him in the parking lot. "Why didn't you kids tell Bo you didn't know how to run an outboard?" he demanded. "You scared Eddie's mother out of her wits."

Mrs. Prince was sunbathing at the pool, and slipped

on a robe and came to meet them. "I'm sorry we worried you, Mom," Eddie said.

"You did," she said, "you gave me an awful fright. Are you going home now, Jay? If you are, I'll give you a ride. Your mother promised me some directions for knitting a sweater. Wait until I get dressed."

They opened the windows of the Prince car, which had been standing in the sun and was like a furnace, and waited in the shade of the marina's sloping roof. Eddie put into words what was on the tip of Jay's tongue to say, "It's great that our folks get along." The Princes and the Sharps had become friends; when Eddie's parents came for a swim they had stayed for a couple of hours to play bridge.

Eddie startled Jay again with his next comment, because again he put into words what was on Jay's mind. "I guess I ought not to keep poking my nose in your business, but I think maybe you've been wrong all along about Mal," Eddie said. "He seems like a pretty good guy."

Mrs. Prince appeared just then, and saved Jay from having to answer.

The subject of buying a boat came up again that weekend, but it wasn't Mal who brought it up. Parents thought they were so smart that their kids couldn't see through them. It was obvious that Mr. and Mrs. Sharp had talked the matter over. "Mal, suppose we go this morning and look at boats," Mr. Sharp suggested casually.

Mal's tone was gruff, and his answer was oddly rude,

"Let's not and say we did." His father dropped the subject.

He brought it up again, though, when he and Jay went together to buy the newspaper and some ice cream on Sunday morning. "I don't know how to say this, Jay," he began. "I've been wondering how you would feel about you and Eddie including Mal in, giving him a part ownership, so he could use your boat."

There was a long silence. They crossed the Riding Way and reached the mainland and stopped for a traffic light. Mr. Sharp tried again. "It's been a source of grief to your mother and me that you boys act as though you actually hate each other," he said. "Oh, I know you have some cause, Jay. Mal is impulsive, and he's walked all over your feelings many times. You boys are so different! You're not careless, you wouldn't hurt a living thing. You take after your mother that way. But you have one serious fault, son. You hold grudges. You can't forgive a hurt. In the years to come, life's going to hand you a great many hurts, Jay."

Jay slid down on his spine. He hated these heart-to-heart talks. If he spoke he might blurt out everything.

How about the time he had been cornered by a bunch of boys in the schoolyard? Mal had seen and walked away, and afterward he had said, "You've got to learn to fight your own battles, kid."

How about the time the elevator in the apartment house got stuck with him and Mal in it? Jay had cried and sobbed in utter terror, and Mal had demanded scornfully, "Are you going to be a baby all your life? Can't you do anything except cry?"

How about the time Jay had started to cross the avenue just as the light changed, darting ahead of Mal into the path of a bus? A cop blew his whistle but Mal got there first, and caught Jay's shoulder and threw him clear. As long as he lived Jay would never forget lying there in the street, a crowd gathering, and Mal yelling, "You brat! You darn stupid brat! The next time I'll let you get hit. The next time I won't risk my neck!" The doorman had come and rescued Jay, blubbering with fright. Mal had stalked away.

If Jay multiplied these incidents by a hundred he would have a pretty accurate count of the number of times his brother had humiliated him.

All this was running through his mind as his father drove on and parked in front of the drugstore. His father waited, but Jay didn't speak, and his father sighed and went to buy his paper.

12

HE HAD TO TAKE a ribbing from Bo and the others when he showed up on Monday. That was the price of having friends, he had discovered; you had to take a lot of kidding. Apparently his and Eddie's wild flight on their maiden voyage had looked even worse from shore than it had seemed to them in the boat.

Mr. Towner caught him and Eddie as they were passing the store and called them into his office and gave them a sharp lecture on boat safety. He made them promise they would never venture out without oars and life preservers.

They didn't say anything. "You can borrow life preservers from your dad's boat, can't you?" he asked. Eddie nodded. "But you haven't any oars?"

The boss shook his head, looking disgusted. "How did I ever get into a deal with a pair of deadbeats like you two?" he asked. "I'll tell Bo to find you a pair of oars, and that's the last free equipment you get out of me. If all my customers were moochers like you, this place would go broke in a week."

Bo complained, too. He found them the oars, but he said gloomily that he was being robbed blind. They must have looked shocked because he added that maybe he wasn't being robbed but everybody felt free to borrow tools from the shop and then forgot to bring them back.

This gave Jay a brilliant idea.

He did his work carefully that morning, giving the area around the office and store a thorough trimming and weeding, picking up even the gum papers and matches. He hauled the hose over and watered the shrubbery. Then he gave the machine shop an extra-special cleaning.

He filled barrels with oil cans and junk, and one of the mechanics helped him roll them outside. Then he swept the floor. His dungarees and T-shirt were a mess by the time noon came. He quit promptly.

He ran into Eddie outside the shop, and explained his great idea, and Eddie was anxious to help. He went home with Jay for lunch. They found Emma in one of her nit-picking moods, but this didn't bother them. Eddie had been at Jay's house often enough to learn to laugh at Emma's moods.

She picked on Jay because his T-shirt was so filthy.

He grandly told her not to worry because he planned to buy some new ones with his next pay. "Humph," she snorted, "you're getting kind of big for your breeches, young man."

It occurred to Jay that earlier, at the beginning of the summer, he would have been hurt if Emma had made a crack at him in front of anybody. Now it didn't bother him; he scarcely noticed it.

He knew there were some cans of spray paint stored in the cellar. His father had used them to freshen up the wicker furniture when they came to the island in June. A couple of cans still had paint in them, a bilious sort of yellow paint that was all right. He and Eddie proceeded to cut small and large stencils out of heavy cardboard.

They put their paint and stencils in a box and set out for the marina. Major set up a howl when he realized that Jay was abandoning him for the second time that day, and Jay freed him and he trotted along with them.

Their luck was in; Bo and the other mechanics were out on a call, bringing in a boat whose engines had failed. The boys had the shop to themselves. They spread papers on the floor, then took all the tools down from the walls and off the benches. They sprayed through their stencils, so that each article read, STOLEN FROM TOWNER'S MARINA. The paint was the fast-drying kind, and they were able to replace all the tools and clean up the mess and leave before Bo and the others returned.

This time, when they got back to Jay's house, his

mother was home. They sneaked up to Jay's room, took off their clothes, and wadded them up to be burned, because besides being filthy they were covered with a fine mist of yellow paint. Luckily, they had covered their hair with the painters' caps Bo kept in the shop. Their skin was slightly yellow, and they had to scrub their faces with scouring powder.

Jay could hardly wait to get to work the next morning, to learn Bo's reaction. He and Eddie were hanging around the store when Bo came running, carrying a handful of small tools, shouting, "Look what some smart guy did!" Nobody could tell him who had done it, and the boys kept mum.

Mrs. Shortley was the detective who found them out. She was laughing when she grabbed Jay by the shoulder and pushed him at Bo. "Here's the smart aleck," she said. "He's still got paint behind his ears!"

Bo thanked Jay and Eddie, pounded their backs, and told them it was the cleverest trick he had ever heard of. "Nobody will swipe my tools again!" he gloated.

Things quieted down and Jay went back to his work. All morning he felt so happy his heart felt swollen in his chest. He was a great one for figuring things out, and while he went from one odd job to another he was thinking. Why was he so happy he felt as though he were suffocating? It was because these people liked him. They really did. He wouldn't have swapped his friendships with Bo, with George, with Mr. Towner, with Mrs. Shortley, for all the riches in the world.

He had lost most of his fear that anybody was going

125

to bust up his friendship with Eddie. It wasn't such a fragile thing that Eddie would throw him over, for Roy or any other kid.

Eddie had a date with his mother for that afternoon. Mrs. Prince said she was ashamed to see her son going around in rags, and she wanted to outfit him with new sneakers, pants, and shirts. The boys planned to meet later. If Eddie got back from the shopping expedition early enough, they could take the *Blue Witch* out for a couple of hours.

As Jay walked home for lunch his happiness went right along with him. The world was a great old place to live in. I've got it made, he thought. I've got a great set of parents and I've got a lot of wonderful friends. And boy, I sure have got me a nice dog. He looked forward to the moment he set foot in the yard, when Major would let out a howl of welcome.

Approaching the south shore, he saw that a sea haze had settled over the Sound. He could make out Littlefield Light, shimmering bluely on the horizon. The sky overhead was brilliantly clear.

Major threw himself on him, begging for a petting. Jay gave his ears and back a good scratching, and held the door open for him.

Mal was in the kitchen. "Where's Mom?" Jay asked.

"She and Emma went to town," Mal told him.

Jay's sharp eyes caught the fact that two places had been set at the table. There were two empty plates and one glass of milk. "Hey," he said, "I bet you ate my lunch."

"I guess I did," Mal said. "Sorry, kid. I was starved."

Jay hesitated. His happiness had exploded like a balloon and he was right back where he had started, behind the eight ball. He was stuck with a brother who was a bully. He was so angry because of the way the joy had gone out of his day, his fists clenched.

Mal was watching his face. "Look, let's not make a big thing of it," he said. "Don't run to Mom like a crybaby when she gets home. I'm sorry. I didn't think. There's plenty of stuff in the pantry, and I'll make you some peanut butter sandwiches, how would that be? Better than the roast beef sandwiches Emma left, I'll say that."

"You ate my roast beef sandwich?"

"It's gone, and there's nobody here but us, so I reckon I must have," Mal said with a laugh. "Any kid who makes as much money as you do at that marina can buy his own lunch. Did you ever think of that? I've got me a couple of jobs, mowing lawns, but I'm not doing as well as you are, Squirt. So you ought to be sorry for your poor old brother, and not begrudge him one measly sandwich."

It was a little thing, but it was an awful big thing, too. Jay was scared, but suddenly, for the first time in his life, he was more angry than scared. He didn't care what happened — he only longed to land a fist in the middle of that teasing, laughing face.

Jay let out a crazy yell and swung, and his fist connected with Mal's nose. His hand hurt and he only

hoped Mal's face hurt, too. He didn't have time to get in another blow. He had no idea how to protect himself and, before he knew how it happened, Mal had caught his wrist and twisted it up behind his back.

He didn't yell, he didn't cry. Mal let go. "Come on, Squirt, hit me some more," Mal ordered.

Jay just stood there, breathing hard. "Come on, Jay, hit me," Mal ordered. "That's been our trouble all along, didn't you know that? You never hit back. Come on, now! Put your left arm up so I can't slug you in the stomach, and hit me again with your right!"

Jay stared at him for a long minute. Then he darted out the door. He was running out of the yard when he heard the door bang, and turned. Mal stood there with a pleading look on his face. "Jay, don't run away!" he begged. "Come on back and let's finish it. I won't hurt you, honest!" Jay kept going.

He felt like blubbering, but he told himself, I'm not going to cry, and he didn't. His heart pounded as he ran, heading away from home toward the place where he could feel safe and happy.

The marina was a busy place on a beautiful summer day, but it seemed empty without Eddie around. Jay idly watched the little kids swimming in the pool, but his mind was still on the scene in the kitchen. He couldn't forget the begging look on Mal's face as Mal urged him to hit back, to stand up on his own feet and defend himself.

He wandered down the front dock and chewed the fat with Hank. He was keeping an eye on the ramp, watching for Eddie.

A familiar voice called, "Hey, Jay!" Larry's runabout was slowly cruising up the channel, and Mal stood in it, waving his arms. Jay didn't wave back.

Larry speeded up. Jay was leaning on a piling, watching the runabout churning a wake, when Eddie appeared beside him. "Wasn't that Mal and Larry?" Eddie asked.

"Yeah," Jay said. "Let's go."

"Okay, just as soon as I help my mother."

He scrambled aboard the *Sara S.* and Jay handed

him the packages from the dockcart. "All right, you two can run along," Mrs. Prince told them.

They were eager to get away, but they thought out their procedure carefully. They didn't want to repeat their first spectacular departure. Eddie loosened the lines. Jay took the tiller, and after he jerked the starter rope and the motor sputtered to life he took a slow course between the dock area and the sailboats bobbing at anchor. When they reached the channel, they had plenty of room.

Safe in the channel, they grinned at each other. "Boy! It makes you feel like a king," Eddie said, and Jay nodded, knowing what Eddie meant. Once you cut the ties to land you were free.

"How about Three Penny?" he asked.

Eddie nodded. Jay steered for the island, skirting the shoals of eelgrass. He slowed the motor. "Let's not go ashore," Eddie said suddenly. "It's great just to be going."

"All right by me," Jay said. "Do you want to take her?"

"No," Eddie said, "you're doing okay, skipper."

13

JAY REJOINED the boats in the channel, keeping the red buoys to his right, watching for sailboats tacking with the wind and for motorboats whose heavy wakes would rock the *Blue Witch*. His happiness had come back. This was the life, he thought. They reached the Spindle, the light on a pile of rocks at the mouth of the river. The whole Sound lay before them.

"I don't want to be a hog," he told Eddie. "You take her now." They changed seats.

This was their first trip on the Sound, and they didn't have a chart or a compass, but who needed them on such a clear day? Eddie really let the motor out and they skimmed over the water, as though they were flying. Eddie was keeping the boat's bow on Littlefield Light, shimmering a couple of miles away. Jay slid over to the bow seat, so he and Eddie faced each other, because he wanted to see how the shore looked, fading away behind them.

He stared over the side, too, into the murky, green depths, and he thought how marvelous it was not to be afraid. He could swim now. He could take care of himself.

"Hey," Eddie said, in a low voice, "look."

Jay swung around and stared. It was hard to believe what was happening. Littlefield Light had vanished. Fog was coming in from the sea, not like a wall gradually moving toward them, but like a giant rug unrolling on top of the water — thick and impenetrable. Eddie didn't think to cut the speed, and they plowed straight into the fog. Immediately the whole world disappeared.

Eddie did cut the speed then. The propeller was hardly spinning. They could just make out a lobster buoy, ten feet away. "Turn it off," Jay suggested.

They listened. In the utter silence they heard only the gentle slap and ripple of waves along the *Blue Witch*'s sides. Then, from far off, came the bellow of the foghorn at Littlefield Light, sounding like a sick cow.

This world was completely unreal. It was like being dropped down a deep, white well. "We'd better start her up and head home," Eddie whispered.

"Yeah," Jay whispered back. "Which way is home?"

"That way." Eddie pointed.

"That's funny," Jay told him. "I'd have said the

132

Spindle was in the other direction. It can't be, though, because Littlefield's over there. At least the foghorn sounds that way."

"I don't think so," Eddie said doubtfully. "It sounds to me like it's coming from the left."

"How far do you think we came after we left the mouth of the river?"

"Not more than half a mile."

It seemed to Jay they had run at least a couple of miles after they passed the Spindle, but he didn't say so. His and Eddie's ideas of their position were exactly opposite. What did it matter, though? They might as well be blind, he thought. Indeed, his eyes did begin to feel queer, staring into the blank fog.

The hoot of a boathorn not far off startled them. Eddie stood up, calling, "Hey, where are you? We're over here." The sea was glassy calm but Eddie's motion set the *Blue Witch* to rocking, and fear gripped Jay. Nobody answered Eddie's call.

Jay was beginning to feel truly afraid. This sea was very deep, and maybe he could swim fifty feet if he had to, but not much farther. The ghostly curtain around them, and the silence, gave him the eerie feeling that he and Eddie were the last two people alive on earth.

Eddie looked pale, too, but he made a joke, "We're a fine pair to get lost at sea — we didn't even bring a chocolate bar!"

Jay tried a brave remark, too, to see how it sounded. "This fog will probably lift any minute, as fast as it came."

This didn't sound as reassuring as he meant it to be. He and Eddie both knew that sometimes the midsummer fogs that blanketed the coast lasted for days.

"Listen," Eddie said. From somewhere came the sound of men's voices. "Hello," Eddie called. "Hello, out there!"

"Where are you?"

"Over here."

"Where's 'over here'?"

"Over here, that's all we know," Eddie called back, sounding desperate.

Jay's ears ached, he was listening so hard. For a while they heard the voices. Then they were gone.

He hesitated to speak, knowing Eddie would realize how scared he was. Finally he croaked, "We're drifting, Eddie. Look at that lobster-pot buoy over there. That stays anchored, but we're moving away. Which way is the tide running? Did you notice, before we left the dock?"

"No." Eddie's voice came out a croak, too.

They were silent for a few minutes, and then Jay tried again, "Do you remember how Mosby Island lies off the mainland? We couldn't drift out to sea without going through Littlefield Channel, or else through the Race, at the other end of Mosby Island." He was trying to find a crumb of comfort for himself. Eddie didn't answer, and Jay said again, "We couldn't drift out to sea, isn't that right, Eddie?"

"How would I know?" Eddie demanded sharply. "I don't know any more than you do. We're just a pair of

134

babes in the woods — we've got no business to be out here. We've got no compass, we've got no nothing! We didn't even mind what Mr. Towner said and bring along the life preservers."

"Well, I was just thinking out loud," Jay muttered. They both listened again to the faint slap of water against the side. Once a fish jumped nearby and they jumped, too, and laughed together shakily.

They drifted for what seemed like hours, scarcely breathing, their ears sticking out, listening. Eddie broke the silence. "Whatever happens, we won't drink sea water," he said in a low voice. Jay hadn't even thought about drinking sea water. "You can go crazy," Eddie explained. "It scrambles your brains."

Jay put up his hand, for he had heard a faraway sound that puzzled him. Eddie cocked an ear, hearing it, too, a heavy rumble that was also a high whine. "That doesn't sound like a boat," Eddie whispered.

"No," Jay whispered back. Then he gave a shout, "It's a truck! That's what it is, a truck in low gear. I saw the town crews this morning mending the roads, getting ready to oil them."

"Sure, that's what it is!" Eddie yelled.

What got into Eddie then to do what he did, he never afterward could explain. He stood up and seized Jay and pummeled his back and hugged him, shouting, "We're okay! We're right on top of our own island . . ."

The *Blue Witch* rocked wildly. Then, very slowly, she turned over.

Jay and Eddie frantically clutched at the boat but it slipped out of their hands. They were thrashing in the water, sputtering and yelling. Jay's head went under and when he came up Eddie had him by the back of his T-shirt. "Make for the boat," Eddie ordered. "Keep moving."

The boat was only twenty feet away, but it was the longest twenty feet in the world. Eddie never let go of Jay's shirt until they were both clinging to the slippery keel. They watched the oars and bailer float away. Jay had swallowed sea water and the thought came to him, now I'll find out if drinking salt water does scramble your brains.

"Try to climb higher," Eddie urged. "Can you make it? Oh gosh, Jay, I'm sorry I threw us in."

"That's okay," Jay said. He gave a heave, so he lay on his stomach across the bottom of the overturned boat.

"You know something? You're okay," Eddie said. "As long as I've got to be shipwrecked, I'm glad it's with you."

They rested, still hearing the far-off noises of a truck backing, shifting gears, dumping its load. With this sound there mingled another. Eddie cocked an ear, listening hard. "It sounds like an outboard, running slow," he whispered.

They still couldn't see, the fog was as thick as ever, but then words drifted through the white curtain. Somebody distinctly said, "My nutty brother."

The next words were louder. "Yeah, he's a nut, all right, and so's the one he pals around with."

Jay yelled, "Mal, Mal, Mal!"

"Hey, do you really think it's your brother?" Eddie cried.

"I know it is. Mal, we're over here!"

The whiteness was parted by the bow of Larry's boat. "Mal, we're over here!" Jay called again.

"Yeah." His brother sounded annoyed. "I can see you." The two boats drifted together.

The older boys roughly pulled Jay and Eddie into Larry's boat. They crouched in the bottom, shivering, watching Larry and Mal struggling to turn the *Blue Witch* over. Mal finally jumped into the water and gave the gunwale a mighty heave and over she went. "You're a great pair of sailors," he said. "You didn't even have a bailer."

"We had one, but it was plastic and it floated away," Eddie explained.

"Yeah, sure," Larry said. "Mal, you dumb oaf, naturally it floated away." He tossed his own over to Mal.

It seemed queer to Jay, hearing his brother called a dumb oaf, but he realized it didn't mean a thing. It was just the way kids talked.

It didn't mean a thing, either, when Mal turned on him fiercely, after Larry had started the motor and set a course for shore, towing the *Blue Witch*. "You and your great boat!" Mal burst out. "Do you know something? Mom's just about out of her skull. She got a call from Eddie's mother and they're both half wild.

138

They think you two are drowned out here. I tried to tell Mom, 'Good riddance,' but oh no! I had to drag Larry out and risk us getting lost, too, because you and your great friend Eddie don't have the sense you were born with!"

Jay was staring right into his brother's face, and he began to laugh. "What's the matter with you?" Mal demanded. "This is no joke!"

Jay stopped. Every once in a while, though, his laughter burst out again.

Soon trees appeared ahead, like ghosts hung with fog, and then the shingle of the beach. The bottom of Larry's boat scraped sand and they scrambled out.

The ground under his feet felt wonderful to Jay, but his legs wobbled. Eddie's acted the same way, and he clutched Jay as they staggered up the beach together.

"You go straight home, Jay," Mal ordered. "Show Mom your ugly mug and let her know you're all right."

"Mal," Jay said, "if you want me to punch your nose, and if you'll stand still, I'll do it."

The other two boys stared at him. It did sound like a crazy remark. Mal understood all right, though, and a grin spread over his face. "Get out of here," he said. "I haven't got time to fight you now. Go along. We'll take care of your boat."

Jay and Eddie scrambled up a low bank and reached the road. Sure enough, the dump truck they had heard out there in the fog came growling along in low gear. It didn't seem possible that only an hour ago they had been drifting, lost and frightened.

Far down the road Jay's mother appeared around a bend, with Major towing her, lunging to reach his master. Jay waved, and broke into a run.

Eddie slowed him down, holding his arm. "Wait," he said. "Stop. I want to say something. I want to tell you, you're an awful fool to let Mal bug you. He went to an awful lot of trouble to find us out there."

"He doesn't bug me." The minute the words were out Jay felt stunned. They were the truth.

"He's okay," Eddie said.

They slowly walked on. "It wouldn't be so terrible if we let him come in with us, and buy a share in the *Blue Witch*," Eddie went on. "I mean, I think he's really a great guy."

Jay felt he was making a very astonishing discovery. He had to try it out in his mind before he put it into words. Two months ago he would have cut his tongue out before he would have admitted such a thing. "Yeah," he said aloud, "maybe Mal's not so bad. Maybe it wouldn't be so terrible if we sell him a share. What'll we sell him, a third? . . . Yeah," Jay said in a very surprised voice, "maybe Mal is okay."